# PESTS
## BATTLE TO THE END

HODDER CHILDREN'S BOOKS

First published in Great Britain in 2022
by Hodder & Stoughton

1 3 5 7 9 10 8 6 4 2

A CIP catalogue record for this book
is available from the British Library.

ISBN 978 1 444 94966 7

Printed and bound in Great Britain by Clays Ltd, Elcograf S.p.A.

The paper and board used in this book are made
from wood from responsible sources.

MIX
Paper from
responsible sources
FSC® C104740

Hodder Children's Books
An imprint of
Hachette Children's Group
Part of Hodder & Stoughton Limited
Carmelite House
50 Victoria Embankment
London EC4Y 0DZ

An Hachette UK Company

www.hachette.co.uk
www.hachettechildrens.co.uk

# The PESTS Test (Part 3)

## Answer these simple questions to find out how pesty you are ...

1. You come across a comic.
Do you:
A) Read it
B) Laugh at the funny pictures
C) Tear it up and make it into
your home

2. Your favourite place to get
food is:
A) A pizza café
B) A burger café
C) Underneath the kitchen table

3. Do you take a bath:
A) Once a day
B) Once a week
C) Never, you prefer to lick
yourself all over

4. Which of these super-powers
would you most like:
A) To be able to fly
B) To be able to teleport
C) To be able to open the fridge

5. To get to sleep do you:
A) Listen to an audio book
B) Read your favourite book
(*PESTS* – obvs)
C) Hang yourself upside down on
your clothes rail

**Read bottom of
page to see what
the results mean**

If you answered all As and Bs STOP READING this book immediately.
You will never be a PEST. If you answered all Cs, congratulations, read on,
you are just the kind of creature P.E.S.T.s. is looking for.

# PESTS VS

DR KRAPOTKIN

STIX

BATZ

WEBBO

THE PLAGUES

BLUE

DUG

MAXIMUS

UNDERLAY

# VERMIN

SIR STING-A-LOT

SHIRLEY

RONNIE
AND REGGIE

WINX

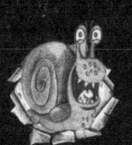

SLY

# GROWING PAINS

This is me, Stix, and thanks to a recent growth spurt, I'm now the height of the tube of Ultra Moisturising Hand Scrub that is next to the sink. Grandma says the mans use it to stop their

paws drying up, which sounds like a very strange thing to me. But then there are lots of odd things the mans do: washing themselves in baths, pushing their babies around in pushchairs and throwing away perfectly tasty food.

The mans we live with are called MyLove, Schnookums and Boo-Boo. I actually quite like them, even though they'd set traps and try and kill us if they knew we lived here too. That might sound mad, but I've known them all my life, so in a way they feel a bit like family — a very odd-looking family, ha!

Schnookums

MyLove

Boo-Boo

Our mans have a dog called Trevor. He's long (like a
sausage) and grumpy (like an old spider), but we are kind
of friends. Which I know sounds weird – me a tiny mouse
and him a big dog – but then nothing about my life is
really ordinary. My best friend is a bat, I go to a secret
school for pesty creatures, and I don't have parents. The
last point is strange and sad at the same time. Grandma
refuses to tell me exactly what happened to them, which I
am sure means that they are gone for ever, and by that
I mean, dead.

Grandma and I live behind the washing machine in the
kitchen of Flat 3, Peewit Mansions, along with the mans
and Trevor (though they don't live behind the washing

machine – they wouldn't fit, ha, ha, ha!). Not so long ago it seemed very possible that we were all going to have to move out. But by using some cunning pesty skills, me and my classmates stopped that from happening. Big PHEW!

Grandma and I sleep all day and when it gets dark we come out to look for food. I play for a while and then go to school. And right now, school is very exciting. Webbo, the spider, says he's heard we are all going to go on a night-trip to the Outside – and he thinks it's going to be to the garden. I have only been to the Outside once in my life, and that was when I fell out of a window (but that's another story) which, I have to say, doesn't really feel like it counts as a proper visit.

Since Webbo mentioned the Outside I've hardly been able to think about anything else. I mean, yes, it might be dangerous but I'm not a baby mouse any more, and I'm ready for some new adventures.

I'm not so sure Grandma is going to feel the same way. She has been cutting me a bit more slack recently, but allowing me to go Outside, that's a whole different block of cheese.

I'm not going to say anything to her yet: I don't want her getting in a Mad Mouse Mood for no reason.

To distract myself I've been working on some NEW SKILLS. That's right, it's not just my body that's grown, it's my abilities too. The other night, when we were searching for food, I did this epic leap from the kitchen table on to the countertop. Honestly, it was HUGE. I was so pleased with myself. Grandma, on the other paw, just let out a long, exasperated sigh; something she's been doing a lot recently.

It goes a bit like this:

I do a skid all the way across the floor on my bottom (a run-up from the living room is required). Grandma sighs.

I somersault into the kitchen sink. Grandma sighs.

I climb up the kitchen blind and scamper along the top ... well, you get the idea.

And, sometimes, there's loud tutting too. To be honest it's not really a big surprise. Grandma is quite possibly the world's most cautious mouse. She has a list of rules as long as MyLove's arm: don't go near Trevor; don't poop in places the mans will see; don't tear open packets; basically, don't do anything dangerous, or fun, ever. I guess I shouldn't really complain – there was a time when I had to hide my skills from her. At least I don't have to do that any more.

Tonight, the mans had curry for dinner. Grandma really likes spicy food, but I don't. So, whilst she clambers up to the sink to see if there are any plates or cooking dishes to lick, I go over to Boo-Boo's highchair to see if she's left anything. I find the foot of a small gingerbread man; it's delicious, and fills me with energy. When I've finished, I find myself bounding across the kitchen floor towards Trevor

– I've suddenly got the urge to leap over his nose. I love jumping over parts of him. I know if Grandma sees me I'll be in trouble. But she's eating in the sink and, honestly, it will only take a couple of seconds.

I time my take-off perfectly. **This is, no doubt, going to be one of my best jumps,** I think, as I soar through the air. But then I look up mid-somersault, and there she is, scowling back down. Eurgh, it's so annoying. It's like Grandma has some special mouse sense that tells her when I'm doing stuff I shouldn't be. What was I thinking? I should have waited until she had gone back to bed.

I land perfectly, but my heart is heavy – I know I'm going to get a right earful. However, just as she opens her mouth to say something there's a tap on the window.

It's Batz! 'Come on,' she mouths, pressing her body against the glass. 'Time for P.E.S.T.S.'

Quick as a flash, I scramble up the kitchen drawers to the sink.

'You know, jumping Trevor is very—'

I skid over to Grandma and plant a big kiss on her cheek. 'Got to go, don't want to get a late mark,' I say, giving her no chance to finish her sentence. I slide down into the sink and scramble over to the plug hole. 'Love you. See you later,' I call out, as I wiggle my body through the hole and into the pipe below.

I feel my body start to slide and, **whoosh**, I'm on my way to school.

# THE MEXICO WORLD CUP '86

**The Peewit Educatorium for Seriously Terrible Scoundrels** — or P.E.S.T.S. as we call it — is a school where pesty creatures, like me, come to learn how to be the best pests we can be. It's in the basement of Peewit Mansions. The route I take there, through Secret Highway Number 2, twists and turns. I slide through pipes and tunnels until, finally, I tumble out on to the basement's dusty floor.

Batz, as always, is waiting for me. I think this is partly

because we are best friends and she wants to see me, and partly because she LOVES to talk and the sooner she sees me the sooner she can fill me in on what she has been up to.

'Boy, it was chaos outside tonight,' she beams, helping me to my feet. 'The garden was chock-full of delicious gnats. It was like the biggest buffet ever.'

I've never told Batz how jealous I am that she gets to go outside. That might well be something to do with the fact that she barely ever lets me get a word in.

'So, how about a quick game?' she continues. 'Tag? Hide and seek?'

'Hide and seek,' I quickly reply. I learned the hard way that playing tag with a creature who can fly is really no fun. 'And I'll hide.'

I'm really good at hiding and she knows it. Grudgingly, she covers her eyes and starts to count. '1 ... 2 ... 3 ...'

I already know where I'm going: I scoped it out the other night. I bound over to the broken vacuum cleaner and quickly wiggle my way into the long, black tube that is hanging out of it.

'Ready or not, here I come,' I hear Batz call.

I hold myself as still as I can. The pipe is full of dust and I'm scared if I breathe it in I'll sneeze, so I hold my breath too. Outside I hear her flitting frantically around, checking in all my usual spots.

'Arghh, I hate playing this game with you,' she cries out in frustration. 'I give up! Where are you?'

'Here,' I gasp, rolling out of the end of the pipe. 'I win again, sucker ...! Get it? Vacuum ... sucker?'

'Next time, we are playing tag,' she huffs, but she doesn't stay cross for long. By the time we reach the wardrobe, which is our classroom, she's back to her usual Batzish-self. 'See ya later, alligator,' she laughs, high-fiving me as I spring off the end of the lamp that helps me get up into the wardrobe.

Around me I hear the happy chatter of my classmates. Underlay the carpet beetle and Blue the fly are playing a very competitive game of I Spy.

'ISpyWithMyBugEyeSomethingThatBeginsWithZed,' gabbles Underlay, smiling smugly at Blue.

Webbo the spider is engaged in a one-way conversation with his incredibly hairy legs. He's trying to coax them into

being even longer and hairier. Which, looking at the length and furriness of them, I'm not sure is possible.

I take my place next to Dug the mole. 'I really hope we get to find out about going Outside tonight,' I say.

'Yeah, me too,' he says, kindly pretending to share my enthusiasm. Going Outside is no big deal for someone who lives in the garden.

'Mini mouse wants to go Outside. The pipsqueak thinks he's got what it takes to cut it, out in the big, wide world.' I turn and see Maximus, the rat. He bounds forward, landing in front of me. 'Well, let me tell you, squirt,' he continues, his face now uncomfortably close to mine, 'it won't be more than a minute before you poop yourself with fear and come running back in crying. Boo-hoo.' He balls his paws and rubs fake tears from his eyes. 'The outdoors is for the big and the brave, not the small and the pathetic.'

'Yeah, Maximus, tell it like it is,' giggles Plague Two, one of the two fleas who live in his fur.

'He'll be just fine,' says Dug, protectively. 'I'll make sure of it.'

'You, you furry doughball?' Maximus laughs. '**Protect** someone?'

'Who are you calling "furry doughball", dude? You looked in the mirror recently?' It's Webbo. He jabs at Maximus's tummy with one of his long, hairy legs.

'It's muscle,' snarls Maximus. 'I'm all muscle. You should have seen the badger I beat up the other night. I got a tear in my ear, he got much worse.' He points to a painful-looking rip at the top of his right ear. We all know he is lying because, not long ago, we watched Maximus's ma nearly twist his ear off. It's not other creatures hurting him, it's his own family.

'Incoming!' cries a shrill voice, calling us to attention. Across the basement swoops our unapologetically potty yet utterly brilliant teacher, Dr Krapotkin – a pigeon with a keen dislike of mans  (they are always shooing her away) and cats (Fluffy, the cat from Flat 4, ate her husband). She glides effortlessly over to the wardrobe, taking her position on the upturned paint tin in front of us.

'Darlinks,' she coos brightly, smoothing down her grey feathers. 'Good evening.'

'Good evening, Dr Krapotkin,' we all chorus back.

'Now ...' She taps her beak with her wing. 'You will all be greatly excited to know that the time has finally come for me to talk to you about our little field trip.'

'I told you! I told you!' whispers Webbo, triumphantly.

I feel my heart start to beat faster.

'This trip will take place in two nights' time,' she smiles. I beam back, unable to believe this is really happening. 'In less than forty-eight hours we shall head to the garden to contest none other than the Mexico World Cup '86.' She finishes her sentence with a joyful clap of her wings.

'Oh, no,' sighs Dug, his body slumping next to mine.

'For those of you NOT familiar with our annual sports evening,' she continues merrily, ignoring Dug's clear lack of enthusiasm, 'I shall explain. Every year we vie for the highly coveted Mexico World Cup '86 trophy.'

'It's not a trophy, it's a manky, old, chipped mug and P.E.S.T.S. have NEVER won it,' harrumphs Dug. 'And are not likely to any time soon. V.E.R.M.I.N. **always** win.'

'V.E.R.M.I.N.?' I say. I've never heard this name before.

'The Valiant Educatorium for Rogue, Mischievous and Impertinent Nasties. They are our sister school in the garden

16

shed, and we shall be competing against them,' explains Dr Krapotkin, enthusiastically. 'Now, I know some of you have your doubts' – she looks pointedly at Dug – 'and have heard stories of our losses from your older siblings, but honestly, darlinks, I do believe this year will be our year. I can feel it in my waters.'

'But V.E.R.M.I.N. are so mean, miss,' protests Dug.

'I concede they are a little on the ... tough side, darlink? ... Life on the Outside can do that to a creature ... but that does not make them unbeatable.'

'But if they already live Outside then that means we are going to be challenging them on their own ground ... That's a home advantage to them,' adds Webbo.

'I am afraid, as the current holders of the trophy, they get to pick. But don't be worrying, like I said' – Dr Krapotkin draws herself up and puffs out her chest with a slight wheeze – 'I am strongly believing it will most definitely be coming home with us this year, so next year we will get to choose.'

'That doesn't help us now, though, does it?' sighs Dug. I've never seen him so down. 'Come on.' I give him a playful nudge. 'It might be fun.'

In fact, I think it's going to be a lot more than fun. I'm going to go into the garden, for the first time EVER. I am sooooo excited.

# PESTY TESTY

It is clear that nothing I can say or do will get Dug out of his grump, so I say no more and turn my attention back to Dr Krapotkin.

'Now, darlinks, for tonight's lesson I would like you to be suggesting or inventing some special pesty skills you could use in the Outside, or more specifically, in the garden. A demonstration would be nice but is not totally necessary,' she coos, her head bobbing eagerly up and down. 'I will give you a moment to think and then, one at a time, in the alphabetical order, show me what you've got!'

With a very cheeky grin Batz performs an impressive swooping dive – first flying up to the ceiling and then tucking her wings tight into her body and diving down. She tells us she is demonstrating how to knock a mobile phone from a mans' hand.

'And where would be the most annoying place for the phone to land?' Dr Krapotkin quizzes her.

'In a swimming pool or a glass of water,' answers Batz, promptly.

'Excellent thinking.' Dr Krapotkin claps enthusiastically. 'Blue, your turn.'

Blue proceeds to do some monumentally loud buzzing, which he informs us would most definitely distract and annoy a mans whilst they were sunbathing.

Next, Dug talks us through how he would use cleverly burrowed tunnels to 'disappear' plants from the garden borders. He tells us his particular targets would be pretty clumps of **Leucanthemum**, patches of

**Heuchera villosa** and, his favourite, the rather expensive **Osteospermum jucundum.**

'Well done, darlink, and impressive use of the Latin names,' commends Dr Krapotkin.

Next up is Maximus, who declares the mere sight of him is enough to strike fear into the mans and send them running back into the house. 'I'd just run past them, getting as close as I could,' he smirks.

'Very pure,' says Dr Krapotkin. 'But also very dangerous.'

'Danger is my middle name,' he replies, proudly.

'No, it's not,' giggles Plague One. 'It's Nigel, after your great grandfather.'

'Shut up!' Maximus hisses, swatting at his shoulder. He shoves his way past me, treading hard on my tail.

As I make my way to the middle of the basement, I can't help but wonder why, after all this time, he's still giving me grief. I had thought, after all we've been through, that he might have changed his mind about me, but clearly not.

I push away the thought and focus back on the class. I have decided that I am going to attempt to show off a new talent, one that I have been trying to perfect during my nightly Stix Skills sessions in the kitchen. To perform it I need to find a long, thin piece of wood. I spot a length of cane poking out of the top of a stack of soil-encrusted plastic plant pots. It's perfect – light and flexible. But I've only ever tried this with a short cocktail stick before – the cane is much longer.

I take four deep breaths – my lucky number – then, clutching the top of the cane in my paws, I lift the whole length of it up off the ground and start to run. I'm heading for the bookshelf. I pick up as much speed as I can, then, just before I reach it, I plant the other end of

the cane hard into the floor. As I feel it arc backwards towards me I leap up, propelling my body forwards. 'The Stix Vault!' I announce loudly, as the cane springs straight again and I'm thrown up into the air.

But then I feel my paws start to slip and find myself flying, not towards the top shelf as I had planned,

but towards the bottom one. I land with a bone-juddering
THUD between two dusty old books. I pick myself up and
look back at my perplexed-looking classmates. 'I'd, er, use

my vaulting skills to reach places mice shouldn't be able to get to,' I say, unable to hide the sense of failure in my voice.

'Epic loser,' Maximus mouths silently, making an 'L' shape with his fingers.

'And what would your intention be once you had reached these hard-to-get-to spots?' asks Dr Krapotkin kindly.

'Er, take a poop?' I reply, nervously. 'Take lots of poops ...?'

'Indeed, darlink, top plan. The more doo-doos the merrier. Mans hate finding poop in unexpected places. Now, Underlay, what have you got for us?'

'I'dNibbleSmallHolesAllOverTheDeckChairs.ImpossibleToMend,' she says. 'NotLikeASimpleTear.'

'An expensive bothering.' Dr Krapotkin nods. 'An excellent idea!'

Finally, Webbo shoots up the side of the wardrobe, showing us the speed he would run up a mans' leg.

'Bonus points if you could make it in all the way to the pants!' cries Dr Krapotkin, clapping her wings enthusiastically. 'Excellent work! You have all made most wonderful suggestions – perhaps some that you will be able to use on Sports Night itself. Now, I am letting you go home early tonight because I need you on tip-top, energetic form for training tomorrow.'

I smile up at Batz. This is just soooo exciting.

'Oh, and darlinks, one last thing ... I need your parents and carers to give permission for you to go Outside. If you could just get their paw or claw mark on this form ...' From under her wing, she produces a small pile of torn-up paper and motions for us all to take a piece.

No! No! No! This can't be happening! I had kind of hoped I could avoid telling Grandma about going Outside. Now, not only have I got to tell her, but I've also got to ask her permission.

I've more chance of opening the fridge door than I have of getting her to agree. She's the Queen of Caution ... This is a disaster, a total and utter **disaster**.

# THE QUEEN OF SUPRISES

Of course, when I get home, Grandma is fast asleep. And there is no way in a trillion years I am waking her – a woken Grandma is a very grumpy Grandma. So, instead, I curl up next to her, and fall asleep trying, desperately, to think of clever things I might say to persuade her to sign the slip.

It must be around lunchtime (I detect the bready smell of sandwiches) when I'm woken by Boo-Boo's loud sobbing. Something must be very wrong: Boo-Boo's crying is rarely loud enough to wake me.

'Mummy, my pho gon,' I hear her wail. 'Me loss it.'

'You've lost your new toy phone, sweetie?' Schnookums replies, softly. 'Don't worry, I'm sure it will turn up. It can't have gone far.'

I drift off back to sleep as Boo-Boo continues to sob. Poor Boo-Boo, I hope Schnookums is right and she finds it soon.

When I wake again, Grandma has already left the nest. I scramble out into the kitchen and spy her over by the fridge. I notice a new drawing stuck to its huge door.

'LOS PHN' I read in Boo-Boo's crayon scribble. Underneath she has drawn a picture of the lost toy and a sad face.

'Evening, my boy,' Grandma smiles. 'Unlike you to sleep in, school must have really worn you out. You got some homework?' she asks, pointing to the permission slip balled up in my paw. 'How about we take a look at it over this delicious lump of chocolate biscuit?' Using her foot she nudges something dry and brown from underneath the fridge. 'Bit dusty, but perfect otherwise. Come on, what are you waiting for?'

I take a deep breath and make my way towards her. This is going to be bad, so bad, bad, bad, I'm sure of it.

'Honestly, my boy, you look like you've swallowed a mouldy prune! Whatever is the matter with you?' she says, handing me a crumb of biscuit.

'It's ... well ... it's not homework,' I say, avoiding her gaze. 'It's a permissionslipformetogoOutside.' I say the words quickly and quietly, in some vain hope this will make my problem go away.

'Did you say, permission slip to go Outside?'

'Yes, for Sports Night,' I mutter, staring furiously at my toes. 'It's fine, I don't expect you to sign it.'

'Well, why ever not? I have a perfectly good paw.' She takes the scrap of paper from me, rubs her paw on the biscuit and places a large, chocolatey smudge in the middle. 'Not terribly legible, but I'm sure it will do,' she smiles.

'You're giving me permission to ... to go Outside?' I am so shocked I can hardly get the words out. She's gone from being the most cautious mouse in the world to the most gung-ho.

'Yes, that's what you asked, isn't it? Is there a reason I shouldn't? Do you not feel capable?'

'I feel very capable,' I quickly reply. 'It's just, well, I thought ...'

'Well, you thought wrong. You're growing up, you need to see more of the world. I will just add a few points of caution.' She takes a deep breath. 'Don't stand in the open, eat ivy berries, or go anywhere near bonfires. Avoid rooks, ravens and crows – they could give you a nasty peck, and owls will kill you. Don't touch anything electric, especially if it is wet. Keep your eyes peeled for the Mogg — they're a nasty bunch of cats, don't usually stalk the garden, but you never know. Hedgehogs are not to be trusted, not in my opinion anyway, and robins, only in an emergency. Stay away from strimmers, leaf-blowers and lawnmowers ... though you don't have to worry if they are turned off. And whatever you do, don't stand out in the rain, as you could get washed down a drain.'

She pauses for breath and smiles. 'I think that just about covers it. Hope I haven't put you off.'

'Er, no ... no ... not at all, that was very informative.' I feel more than a little overwhelmed by the overload of information.

'Well, let's get on and find some more food. Sports Night can really zap one's energy.' And with that, she directs me to the biggest grape I have ever seen.

I end up eating so much that I have trouble fitting through the plug hole.

Tonight, Batz is not waiting. In fact she doesn't catch up

with me until I am almost at the wardrobe.

'Sorry, I'm late,' she says, swooping down next to me. 'I just had the worst sleep ever. Some stupid creatures got up into the loft and were scratching and scrabbling around. Honestly, whoever it was woke me about ten times, no, make that twelve ... thirteen even ...'

I want to tell her that I got woken up too, but she doesn't stop talking until we reach the wardrobe. That's the problem with having a chatterbox best friend.

'Darlinks! Darlinks,' coos Dr Krapotkin excitedly as we take our places on the wardrobe floor. 'First things first, your permission slips, please.' I cheerily add mine to the pile, on top of Dug's. It's hard to tell if anyone signed his, or if it's just covered in mud. 'Magnificent – it looks like you are all on the team. Now, second things second: preparation. We have one more night before the BIG night. The challenges of Sports Night vary from year to year, so you will need to be physically ready for ANYTHING. Which means tonight, darlinks, we shall TRAIN!'

By 'train' it quickly becomes clear she means spend the evening exhausting ourselves. After five laps of the basement (one for Underlay and Webbo, because they are so small, and ten for Batz and Blue as they have the unfair advantage of being able to fly), we are split into groups.

The Flyers: Batz and Blue

The Furries: Dug, Maximus and me

The Chompy-Spinners: Webbo and Underlay.

Each group is given a 'tailored' set of exercises that supposedly plays to our strengths. First up, us Furries have 'endurance training', which means pushing a box of old records (these strange, large, black discs) from one side of the basement to the other. This most definitely plays to Maximus's strengths. However, halfway across he declares he is done making us look good and Dug and I have to push the box the rest of the way on our own. Luckily it turns out Dug is no slouch in the strength department, either. 'Tunnellers' arms,' he

points out proudly as, after a lot of huffing and puffing, we finally get the box across.

Next, we must shred a pile of musty newspapers – much more up my street. But soon after we start, some dust gets up my nose and I explode into a sneezing fit that I just can't stop. Maximus declares himself the winner even though, as Dug points out, it's NOT a competition.

'Honestly, I don't know why we are doing this,' Dug says, as we make our way across to the 'assaulting course' that Dr Krapotkin has built for us. 'We're not just going to lose, we are going to lose badly. Embarrassingly badly.'

After what turns out to be a disastrous lap of the assaulting course – Dug gets caught up in the crawl (fishing) net, Maximus knocks over the pile of boxes that has been set up as a climbing wall, and I misjudge my leap between the microwave and the bookshelf (the thought of Professor Armageddon, the evil cockroach who used the microwave as his home, puts me off my stride) – I have to admit that I think Dug might be right.

We don't stand a chance.

As we gather back in the wardrobe everyone looks as despondent as I feel. All, that is, except Dr Krapotkin, who merrily declares she believes totally and wholeheartedly that we will win. 'This is OUR year,' she proudly reiterates, before dismissing us for the evening.

'She sayzzz that to every clazzz,' says Blue, as we wearily make our way back home. 'My zzzeven hundred and zzzixty zzzecond couzzzzzin told me pezzzts hazzzz never wonzzzz, not wunzzzze.'

# MR MOTIVATOR

I get back to the kitchen feeling extremely tired and rather dejected. What once felt like something really exciting now feels like something very daunting. I drag my weary body back across the kitchen.

'Mouse!' I'm clearly not paying attention to where I am going as I've bumped into Trevor. He blinks open a sleepy eye. 'What going on, mouse?'

'Sorry,' I reply, hastily. 'I didn't mean to wake you.'

'Hmmm, you look worried, mouse,' he says, his manner shifting from grumpy to concerned. 'You OK?'

'Oh, Trevor, not really,' I blurt, as the urge to unburden all that I am feeling overcomes me. 'It's school Sports

Night tomorrow evening and we P.E.S.T.S. are rubbish! We're never going to win. And on top of that it's in the garden, which seems like a place jam-packed with danger. I'll probably get eaten by an owl or washed away in a rainstorm.'

'Woah, mouse, calm down,' Trevor woofs, clambering to his feet. 'Trevor know just what you need.'

'Er, you do?' I say, trying not to sound rude.

What possible help could a dog offer me?

'Yes, mouse need to use positive affirmations, they help soothe the troubled soul,' he replies earnestly. 'Every morning Trevor listen to *Think Yourself Brilliant* podcast with Dr Jason Blossombumm. MyLove put it on before he go to work. Dr Jason Blossombumm very wise. He say ...' Trevor clears his throat and then, in a very calm and

much deeper voice continues, 'When life throws problems in your path, you must see them not as obstacles but as challenges. Nothing is so bad that it cannot be overcome with the power of positive thought.'

He's using a strange accent too. I stifle a giggle as he asks me to repeat his words. 'Say after me ...' he instructs, his voice going lower and his funny accent getting even stronger, 'no problem is so big it cannot be overcome.'

'No problem is so big it cannot be overcome,' I mumble, feeling rather silly.

'I will not allow negative thoughts to drain my energy.'

I repeat sentence after sentence: 'Positive thoughts create positive things. You only fail if you quit. Opinions don't define your reality.' And slowly, incredibly, I start to feel better. Until, by the time he finishes with a mighty, booming: 'I will not let the light of courage dim inside me!' I am not just looking forward to Sports Night but believe we have every chance of winning.

'Thanks, Trevor,' I say. 'That was really helpful.'

'Don't thank Trevor,' he smiles, lying back down. 'Thank Dr Jason Blossombumm.'

I head off to bed and fall quickly into a long, exhausted sleep.


When it comes to time to get up, Grandma has to wake me. 'Stix, Stix,' she says gently, nudging me. 'Stix, come on, it's your big night. I know dear Dr Krapotkin has high hopes for you. Let's make sure you have had enough to eat before you head off.'

It appears, from the debris under Boo-Boo's chair, that she did not enjoy her baked potato with cheese and beans.

'Perfect. Chock-full of carbohydrates,' says Grandma, handing me a delicious lump.

I notice Boo-Boo has added another picture of her lost toy phone to the fridge. This time it is offering a 'rewod' of '1000000000 nanas' — by which I think she means, judging by the yellow shapes all over the paper, bananas.

Grandma finishes her food and then, with a loud yawn, declares she is stuffed full as a sack of spuds and in need of a lie down.

'Now, you go out there and do your best, my boy,' she says, wrapping me in a warm embrace. 'There was a time, not long ago, that I wouldn't have let you out of my sight, let alone out into the garden. But things have changed: I can see what a strong young mouse you're becoming. Just trust those senses of yours and come back to me safe and sound.' She plants a huge kiss on my cheek, gives me one last squeeze and scuttles off back to our nest.

Her words leave me momentarily stunned. Oh, how things have changed! To think Grandma now believes in me. All I have to do now is prove that she's right — eeek!

I look across at the sleeping, snoring Trevor. **We CAN do this**, I think. **We MUST**. I just need to convince my classmates.

I slide down the hidden highway, planning just what I will say. However, the first and only thing Batz wants to talk to me about is the creatures that have been rampaging around the roof cavity, keeping her awake again.

'My fourth cousin on my pa's side of the family, Cedrix,

said he saw something grey and furry. And my Auntie Patz said she saw a tail, a large bushy tail. But no one has actually seen the whole creature. It's a real mystery, a proper puzzle!' She chatters like this all the way to the wardrobe, where we find everyone but Dr Krapotkin is sitting ready for class. They all look glum, even Maximus.

As Batz hangs herself on the clothes rail I take my opportunity to say something.

'So, I've been thinking about Sports Night,' I begin, taking my position in front of Dr Krapotkin's paint tin. I lower my voice just as Trevor did, and adopt his calm tone. 'I know it's going to be tough, but we can't let negative thoughts drain our positive spirit. We haven't failed yet, so why are we behaving like we have?'

My classmates stare back at me blankly.

'We mustn't let the light of courage fade inside us,' I continue, now slowing my words down, trying to remember exactly how Trevor sounded. For a moment I think it's starting to work, but then ...

'Dude, have you eaten a dictionary? You're talking awfully strange,' Webbo frowns. Under my fur I feel myself blush.

'OK, OK, I know it sounds weird,' I say, swapping back to my usual voice, 'but we are mightier than we think. Batz, you're so quick. Dug, you're strong. Webbo, you have eight legs, that's got to be some kind of advantage. Blue, you're loud and zippy. Underlay, you can destroy pretty much anything and Maximus ...'

Maximus glares at me; I notice he now has a rip in his other ear. 'You're brave.'

'Yes, I am,' he smiles, puffing up his chest.

'And you, Stix dear, are extremely wise!' cries Dr Krapotkin, swooping in. 'We, darlinks, are P.E.S.T.S., and that means we have learnt to be the best at being the worst. Do not for one single millisecond doubt yourselves! Do not for one heartbeat imagine anyone else but yourselves raising that trophy.' As she speaks, tears begin to pool in the corners of her eyes. 'I want you to go out there and give those V.E.R.M.I.N. hell — show them the tough stuff you are made of. As they say, it's not over till the fat pigeon sings, and this pigeon sure isn't belting out a tune any time soon.' She balls her wing into a large fist and clutches it to her chest, tears now flowing down both her checks. 'To the garden, my darlinks, to the garden and sweet, sweet victory!'

And with that, she leads us across the basement, her feathers fluffed into a puff ball and her eyes glinting with excitement.

# THE GARDEN!
# I'M IN THE
# GARDEN!

Our route to the Outside is through an air vent at the top of the basement wall. An old wooden ladder helps those of us that can't fly to reach it. As I wiggle my way between the vent's metal bars, a strange tingling sensation fills my body. It travels from the end of my nose to the tip of my tail. I am SO excited. I know Grandma warned of many (bit of an understatement) dangers but, like she said, I'm a big mouse now, I just need to keep my senses about me and I'll be ...

'WOAH!!!!!!!!!!!!!!' I tumble out of the air vent and fall to the ground the other side. I look up and ... **OH MY GOODNESS ... HOLY MOLY ...**

There are no walls, no ceiling — just vast, vast openness. The only light comes from the moon, which casts eerie, long shadows.

I've always felt small, but now I feel microscopic — like a speck of dust on the world's biggest rug. My brain goes into crazy overdrive trying to process the array of foreign smells.

'Oh, wow!' Webbo laughs, pointing at my whiskers. 'It looks as if they're having their own private disco on your face.'

I try to get them back under control as I take everything in. Even the air feels huge. I take a deep breath, filling my lungs with its cool freshness. Then, suddenly remembering where I am, and the danger I could be in, I flatten myself against the concrete ground and switch my nose to CSM (**Constant Sniff Mode**). But all I detect is a strong earthy smell, like the mud on MyLove's running shoes, only a billion times stronger.

'Stix, darlink, come along now, stop all that mouse nonsense.' I hear Dr Krapotkin tut. I look up just in time to see my classmates disappearing into the vast carpet of green that stretches out in front of me.

'It's just grass,' chuckles Batz, doubling back to fetch me. 'It won't bite.'

'Yeah, come on, don't you worry. Just follow me, I'll trample a path for you,' calls Dug.

The grass is tall and slightly damp. It brushes against me like long, cold fingers as I run to catch up with him. He's surprisingly fast for someone with such short legs.

Above me I hear Batz chattering away, excitedly pointing out all the places she knows. 'There's the apple tree where the tasty gnats are, and just over there by the rhododendron bush, that's where I learnt to fly, and over there by the compost heap—'

'Batz,' I interrupt, trying to sound as polite as I can, 'this is really interesting, but all I can see from down here is Dug's bottom.'

'Oh, yes, silly me ... Ha, ha! Well, you'll be pleased to know we are just passing by the funny ornament, which means we're almost there.'

I look up and see an odd creature made of stone looming out of the grass beside us. Balanced on its nose is a large ball.

'It's a seal,' Dug informs me. 'Been here since way before my family came to the garden.'

At last the grass gives way to concrete – concrete peppered with furry lumps of green. 'Moss,' Dug says, poking a lump of it with his toe. 'Or **Bryophyta**, to give it its proper name.' He smiles proudly, clearly enjoying his role as garden guide.

We are standing in front of a huge wooden structure. From the strong smell of decomposing wood, I can tell that it is old and disused.

I notice, nailed near the top of it, a rusted square of

metal. Stamped into it I read the words VALIANT SHEDS.

Dr Krapotkin glides down, depositing Underlay and Webbo next to her.

'ThanksForTheRideMiss,' says Underlay appreciatively. 'WouldHaveTakenAllNightWithoutYou.'

'My pleasure, darlink. Now, Maximus, why don't you do the honours and use that big fist of yours to alert our rivals we have arrived?'

Maximus balls his paw into a fist and then stops, as if confused about what to do next.

'She means bang on the door, you big doofus' I hear Plague One laugh, cruelly.

'Yeah, yeah, I knew that,' Maximus growls, stepping forward.

I almost feel sorry for him: I'd hate to have two nasty fleas like the Plagues mocking me all the time.

He thumps three times on the door. For a moment there is silence, then, just as he raises his fist to bang again, one of the rotten panels of wood creaks, and a small flap at the bottom of it falls open.

'Enter,' commands a voice from inside.

My heart starts to pound. This is it, we are finally going to meet our fearsome opponents. I glance up at Batz; I can tell she's nervous too. In fact, I think we all are. All apart from Dr Krapotkin.

'Come on, darlinks, what are you waiting for?' she says, pushing past us and forcing herself through the small gap.

One by one we nervously follow.

'It zzzzmellz like funguzzz,' declares Blue.

'Yeah, this is the last place I'd want to cast a web,' whispers Webbo.

The inside of the shed is just as rotten and tatty as the outside. It is dank and dark, and immediately gives me

the creeps. Above us shelves slant this way and that, laden with old jam jars and tins. Strange, rusty objects hang from the walls. The floor, which I think was once wood, is now a kind of earthy mush.

'Welcome to V.E.R.M.I.N.,' booms a voice from the far corner.

'I see you've done little to improve the place since my last visit,' says Dr Krapotkin, ushering us towards a strange-looking machine. 'Still using that rust-bucket of a lawnmower as a classroom too.'

My stomach lurches as I begin to make out the shadowy shapes of other creatures. One by one they slowly climb out of the mower ... **But, hold on ... this isn't so bad.**

The tallest are no larger than Maximus.

'Two squirrels, a snail, a hamster and a dormouse,' whispers Dug under his breath. 'Well, this is nowhere near as bad as I imagined. Maybe you're right, Stix ... maybe we **do** have a chance of beating this bunch.'

# V.E.R.M.I.N.

I can't help but stare at the dormouse. She is sort of like me and Grandma, and sort of not. Her fur is a golden red colour – not grey like ours. She is rounder than us and her tail is fluffy, unlike ours, which are bare.

She stares back at me, giving me the kind of look you'd give a foul-smelling lump of rotten food.

From out of the mower buzzes a small black and yellow insect.

'Ah, Sir Sting-A-Lot. There you are, you waspish devil,' coos Dr Krapotkin. Something about the tone of her voice tells me she is not overly fond of him.

'Krapotkin,' he sneers, landing on top of a wobbly stack of plant pots. 'Lovely to see your pigeonish self too.'

They both stare at each other.

'Well, I've already cleared a spot in the basement for the trophy to sit,' says Dr Krapotkin, finally breaking the silence. 'All we need to do now is give you a thorough thrashing.'

'You? Thrash us?' The hamster growls, its voice gruff and incredibly deep. 'Pull the other one. You puny lot'd struggle to beat an egg.'

'Now, now, Shirley,' Sir Sting-A-Lot smiles. 'No need to stoop to their petty level of goading.'

'Shirley?' whispers Webbo.

'Yeah, the name's Shirley,' growls the hamster. 'Pet shop thought I was a girl.'

'YouCouldAlwaysChangeIt,' adds Underlay, helpfully.

'And **why** would I want to do that?' Shirley sounds offended. Something I am very sure we DO NOT want him to be.

'AbsolutelyNoReasonAtAll,' replies Underlay brightly, clearly sensing the danger too.

'OK, come on now, darlinks. Sports Night is about action, not words,' says Dr Krapotkin cheerily.

'Yes, just you wait till you see us in motion,' whispers the snail, staring up at us, his eyes narrowing.

'Don't you mean slow motion?' chuckles Webbo under his breath. 'Snail's pace?'

'What did you just say?' hisses the snail. We all spin around to find him suddenly behind us.

'I am Sly,' he whispers darkly, 'and I am everywhere, and I am nowhere.'

The two squirrels seem particularly interested in Maximus.

'Oi ... you!' whispers one.

'Yeah, you, Big Nose,' titters the other.

'I'm a rat. Rats have big noses,' Maximus snarls back.

'You hear that, Ronnie? He says he's a rat.'

'And there was me thinking he was a horse, Reggie. Ha, ha, ha! A horse, that's a good one. Though I ain't seen no horse with ripped-up ears like that. What happened? You got in a fight with your mum? I heard you rats like a bit of a family scrap.'

Maximus furiously mutters something under his breath, which the squirrels take as their cue to press their faces even closer.

'Hey! Leave him alone.' I find myself stepping forwards. 'What happened to his ears is his business and no one else's.'

'Oooh, look, he's got a mouse for a bodyguard,' smirks Reggie, taking a step back.

'That's enough now,' snaps Dr Krapotkin. 'Sir Sting-A-Lot, call your pupils to order right now!'

Maximus glares at me, clearly embarrassed by the whole situation.

'All right, twins, enough,' says Sir Sting-A-Lot, rolling his eyes. 'How about we all go and view the magnificent trophy. You might as well see what you are about to lose ... again.' He buzzes off into the darkness, beckoning us to follow him.

'Oi, I don't remember asking you to stick up for me,' grumbles Maximus, jabbing me with a sharp claw.

'In case you haven't noticed we're a team, and that means we look out for each other.' I stare him straight in the eye. I'm beyond tired of Maximus always being so horrible. I brace myself for a nasty response or, worse, some pain. But to my surprise he simply replies, 'Well, don't do it again, I don't need your help,' and sulks off ahead.

I feel something bump against me and turn to see the dormouse. 'That wasn't intentional, I slipped,' she says slowly, her voice flat and lacking any energy. 'So, don't read anything into it. It's not like I want to be your friend, all right?'

'Um, OK,' I reply. 'Sure, I mean, fine, I mean, I wasn't expecting you to be.' She doesn't respond but continues to look at me coldly. Is she waiting for me to say more? 'Just because we're both mice, I know that doesn't mean ... you know ... we're going to have anything in common.' What am I doing? It's like her lack of talking is making me talk more.

'You are a **house mouse**.' She says the words like they are some kind of terrible disease. 'We have absolutely nothing in common.' She lets out a sleepy yawn and falls into line with Ronnie and Reggie.

'Cool, cool. Totally get it, no problemo,' I say, far too enthusiastically.

'See you've met Winx.' It's Sly, who's popped up next to me from out of nowhere.

'Winx?' I reply. 'That's an interesting name.'

'Like, "forty winks". Dormice sleep about six months of the year. She could crash out at any moment.'

'That would explain a lot,' I say. 'She does seem pretty drows—' But I don't bother finishing my sentence because I realise Sly has vanished.

We reach an upturned wooden crate at the end of the shed. On top stands a rather chipped, very coffee-stained mug. 'Behold the magnificence of the Mexico World Cup '86,' announces Sir Sting-A-Lot proudly. '**Our** trophy.'

V.E.R.M.I.N. proudly take their place beside him. Ronnie and Reggie glare at us threateningly and Shirley reaches into his cheek and pulls out an enormous energy bar.

'Hey, that's an unfair advantage,' says Dug, as Shirley proceeds to break it up into chunks and hand it to his classmates.

'You're just jealous 'cos you don't have one,' Shirley grins. 'Well, guess what' – he reaches into his other pouch – 'I got two.' He pulls out another and starts to chomp on it himself. 'You'll be amazed what I can fit in these pouches.'

'Don't worry, darlinks, you don't need any fancy-pants stuff to help you win,' says Dr Krapotkin, puffing up her chest. 'There is no substitute for the pure skill. Now, come along, let's get this competition on the road.'

I so want to believe she is right, that we have what it takes. But as I watch V.E.R.M.I.N. standing in front of us, aggressively chomping away, I'm not feeling quite as sure as I was.

'Dudes, prepare yourselves,' whispers Webbo, nervously. 'I think we're about to get a ma-hu-sive whupping.'

# LET THE
# GAMES BEGIN

'We are P.E.S.T.S., we can do this,' I repeat under my
breath as Dr Krapotkin ushers us back out of the shed. If
it can work for MyLove, it can work for me.

'Not that funny mumbo-jumbo again,' says Webbo, rolling
all four of his eyes.

Sir Sting-A-Lot instructs us to take our place in the
'starting pen' – the slab of concrete in front of the shed.
We split into our teams and V.E.R.M.I.N. immediately start
doing some vigorous stretching. Even Sly gets in on the act,
disappearing in and out of his shell with lightning speed.

'OK, so, as protocol dictates, I have written out the twenty challenges that make up this tournament.' Dr Krapotkin pulls a bundle of small, folded pieces of paper out from under her wing.

'TWENTY?' Dug blurts.

'Four shall be chosen at random,' she continues, depositing her paper bundle into an empty flowerpot.

'I really hope there's one that involves burnin' down the pet shop,' Shirley grins.

'And one where we get to nick a motor,' says Ronnie, rubbing her paws together excitedly.

'We are pests, not vandals,' Dr Krapotkin tuts, disapprovingly. 'Now, before we begin, let us get the rules of engagement nice and straight. There shall be' – she turns to face V.E.R.M.I.N. – 'no biting, no scratching, no interfering with your opponents, and no cheating.'

'Boring,' yawns Winx, rolling her sleepy eyes.

'Yes, yes ... blah, blah, we all know the drill,' says Sir Sting-A-Lot, buzzing over to the plant pot holding the challenges. 'Let's just get on with it, shall we? We've only got till sunrise.' And with that he disappears inside, reappearing seconds later holding a slip of paper.

'Challenge one,' he declares, unfolding it. 'NICK IT IN A TICK. The winner of this challenge will be the school that brings back something the mans will **really** miss. You have five minutes starting from ... NOW.'

Quick as a flash, V.E.R.M.I.N. are gone. I can't believe they have thought of something so fast.

'Well, anyone got any bright ideas?' asks Maximus.

'I know where there's a rusty old trowel without a handle,' offers Dug.

'Dude, he said something the mans are going to miss, not something they mislaid and forgot about,' sighs Webbo.

'I know where there'zzz a big dogzzz poo?' Blue shrugs.

'NoOneIsGoingToMissThat,' Underlay babbles.

'I've got a good idea,' says Batz. 'That mans Tarquin from Flat 4 keeps a fancy pair of yellow rubber shoes over by the back door. Ma says he wears them when he comes out to do his meditation.'

'Sounds like a good plan,' I nod, thinking back to how angry MyLove got when he couldn't find one of his slippers the other day.

'All right then, show us the way,' says Maximus. 'I'll take Underlay. Bat – I mean, Batz – you take Webbo.'

'Ooh, get him. He's gone all Sergeant Bossy Boots on us,' Plague One giggles.

'More like Major Muppet,' Plague Two sniggers.

After an exhausting sprint all the way back to the

building, we reach the back door. Just as Batz said, sitting neatly on the top step are a pair of large yellow shoes.

Maximus bounds over and lifts one up. 'Nice and light,' he declares. 'I'll take the left, you bunch of tragic loo—I mean, teammates' – he quickly corrects himself – 'you take the right.' And with that he picks up a shoe, lofts it above his head and disappears back across the lawn.

'How about you take the heel, Stix, and I'll take the toe? Batz, you help him hold it up,' says Dug.

'AndWebboAndIWillGuideYou,' says Underlay, jumping up on to the front of the shoe.

'And I'll give you aerial zzzzupport,' adds Blue.
The shoe isn't too heavy but holding it above my head

soon makes my arms ache. I'm glad I've got Batz and Dug to help me.

'Left a bit, left a bit, nearly there,' encourages Webbo.

'Juzzt a couple more meterszzzz,' calls Blue and, seconds later, I'm relieved to feel my feet touch cold, hard concrete.

Puffing and panting, we drop the shoe next to the one Maximus has already deposited at Dr Krapotkin's feet.

'Brilliant work, darlinks,' she says, clapping. 'Let's see V.E.R.M.I.N. beat that.'

I look at the two, large shoes. We have done well. But then ...

'You've got to be kidding me,' Batz gasps, pointing across the garden.

Coming towards us, balanced on top of a pair of strange-looking boots with wheels, is a television. Ronnie and Reggie pull it along, whilst Winx and Shirley stand on top of it, guiding them.

'But ... **how?**' Webbo blurts, all four of his eyebrows furrowing into a very wiggly line.

'Told ya we can nick anyfink,' says Ronnie with a cheeky

smile. She and Reggie carefully take the television from the boots and place it next to our pair of shoes. With a flamboyant flourish, Shirley proudly pulls the remote control out of his left cheek.

'4K ULTRA HD,' proclaims Sly, slithering his way off the TV's shiny black screen.

'Drat,' mutters Dr Krapotkin.

'Well, I think we have a clear winner, don't you?' Sir Sting-A-Lot grins. 'V.E.R.M.I.N., 1; P.E.S.T.S., nil.'

Maximus looks furious, which I can tell is giving V.E.R.M.I.N. a lot of pleasure. 'I just want to beat them so badly,' he mutters under his breath. Perhaps them being mean to him earlier wasn't such a bad thing after all.

'Well, I don't think that's possible,' Dug sighs, dejectedly. 'We should concede ... give up now.'

'Look, we've overcome bigger hurdles than this,' I say. 'Remember that crazy cockroach, Professor Armageddon, the one who wanted to blow up the block? We stopped him, and that man Colin and his horrific dog who wanted to turn the place into a pesticide factory – we stopped them too. We are better than we think! Come on, we just got off to a bad start ... we'll win the next one, you'll see.'

'OK, darlinks, challenge number two,' says Dr Krapotkin, reaching into the pot. She clears her throat: 'WHOOP-DI-POOP. The winner of this challenge will be the team that poops in the most inappropriate place, and just for added difficulty, you can NOT leave the garden. Points will be given for both size and cunningness of placing.'

This time V.E.R.M.I.N. don't run off, but instead immediately huddle together and begin discussing options.

'OK, then,' whispers Batz, as we too gather in a circle. 'First up, who's the biggest pooper? And I'm afraid you'll have to count me out ... I've already been tonight.'

'It'z not me, zzzatz for sure,' says Blue.

'NotMeEither,' Underlay adds.

'It's got to be between Maximus and Dug, right?' says Webbo. 'I mean, they've got the biggest bottoms.'

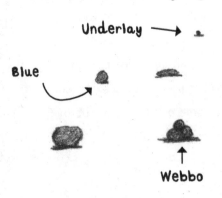

Underlay ⟶

Blue

Webbo ↑

'My bottom might be large, but my poop is rather small,' Dug whispers, apologetically.

'Well, mine are massive,' Maximus declares loudly.

Batz

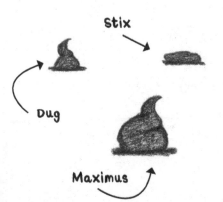

'I'm the poo king.'

'OK, OK, keep your voice down! We don't want to give anything away,' Batz tuts. 'Now, next up, we need to decide where King Poop here is gonna go. Suggestions ...?'

From the sound of the excited voices coming from V.E.R.M.I.N.'s huddle it's clear their planning is going well.

'It's hard to see what options we have from down here,' I say, staring out at the tall grass. I look at Batz. 'How about you and Blue have a quick look around?'

'Plan,' she nods.

Within less than a minute they're back. 'We got a rotten bench hidden in the ivy,' she pants.

'A ruzzzty table,' adds Blue.

'A couple of old plastic chairs, a tired-looking trampoline and a BBQ,' Batz concludes.

Stix

Dug

Maximus

'Got to be the BBQ,' says Maximus. 'No mans wants to open up the cover and find poop on their grill.'

'Hate to say it, but he's got a point,' Batz agrees.

73

'Great!' Maximus replies, bounding off across the garden. 'One mega dump coming right up.'

I check around the garden trying to see where V.E.R.M.I.N. have gone. 'They're over there, by the trampoline,' says Batz excitedly. 'No one's used it for years. Think you might be right about us winning this one.'

Maximus comes galloping back looking very pleased with himself. 'I laid a whopper, as big as an egg,' he declares, triumphantly.

Winx, Sly and Shirley soon return looking very pleased with themselves too.

'So, who would like to be the first to tell us what awfulness they have done?' says Dr Krapotkin.

Dug's large paw immediately shoots up. 'The BBQ,' he blurts. 'Maximus did a big one on the grill.'

Next to him Maximus puffs out his chest, grinning proudly. Sir Sting-A-Lot zips over to the BBQ and returns a short while later confirming, in a deeply annoyed manner, that Maximus has indeed done very well.

'Excellent.' Dr Krapotkin claps, unable to hide her pride.

'V.E.R.M.I.N., let us see if you can beat THAT!'

'We did one on the trampoline,' Winx says, flatly.

'Well, I think the winner of this challenge is most clear then,' Dr Krapotkin beams. 'The trampoline is never used, I declare P.E.S.T.S. are the wi—'

'—But that's not all,' Winx interrupts. 'If you would

please ...' She directs our gaze to the strange-looking structure Batz just pointed out to me. Silhouetted, on top of the fence next to it, I see Ronnie and Reggie. They've somehow managed to wrestle the seal's stone ball up there too.

'How on earth ...?' gasps Batz.

But before anyone has time to answer, Ronnie and Reggie have pushed the round object off the fence. It drops on to the trampoline and, with a loud BOING, catapults a lump of something large and poo-shaped high up into the air.

We all stand and watch in stunned amazement as the poo flies across the night sky towards the mansion block.

'And if we have the trajectory correct,' says Winx, tracing its path with her finger, 'it should go straight into—'

We let out a collective gasp as the poo sails, with unbelievable precision, through an open window on the fourth floor.

'—Tarquin's flat,' says Batz, finishing her sentence for her.

'Exactamundo,' says Shirley, triumphantly. 'A poop in the

bedroom, maximum point-idge to us.'

   'B ... but the rules said we couldn't leave the garden,'

Maximus stammers furiously.

'Well, we didn't,' Sly smiles. 'Only the poo did.'

Dr Krapotkin lets out a long, defeated sigh.

'OK, **now** I agree with you,' I whisper to Dug. 'I think we should give up.'

# DOWN BUT NOT OUT

Losing feels horrible, like someone has taken every ounce of joyful feeling I have and stamped all over it. The Outside doesn't feel exciting any more. It feels difficult

and depressing. I want to go home. But if I do I'll have to face Grandma, and I'll have to tell her I gave up. Which, given all the faith and trust she puts in me, feels like an even worse thing than staying here and getting beaten.

I can tell from the look on my classmates' faces that they feel equally deflated.

'Just two more challenges to go,' says Sir Sting-A-Lot gleefully, diving into the flowerpot once more. 'And if V.E.R.M.I.N. win this one then it's 3-0, and game over.'

'Yes, yes, thank you, we can count,' snaps Dr Krapotkin angrily. I feel bad about her too; I know how much winning this would have meant.

'So, the third challenge,' Sir Sting-A-Lot beams, unfolding the strip of paper gripped in his claws. 'BURY IT IN A HURRY — either bury an item of the mans, or, in case you have already selected the NICK IT IN A TICK challenge ...' Sir Sting-A-Lot's face suddenly drops: '... bury that item instead.'

'Fastest team wins,' Dr Krapotkin cries, with newfound enthusiasm. 'Go, darlinks, GO!'

I look from the yellow shoes to the huge TV.

'Unless they've got a digging machine hidden somewhere, we've got this,' says Dug, his face breaking into a huge grin. 'You grab the shoes – I know just the place to bury them.'

Maximus takes one, and Batz and I half carry, half drag the other. Luckily Dug hasn't gone far. When we reach him, he's already scooped out a reasonable-sized hole. 'They used to dump the compost here,' he says, clods of earth flying up around him. 'Means the soil is nice and soft.'

Maximus and I jump in the hole and start frantically digging alongside him. In no time at all we've dug out a space easily big enough to fit the shoes. We drag them in and then quickly pile the soil back on top. 'And a chunk of turf for good measure,' says Dug, placing a lump of grass on top of the bare soil.

'FINISHED,' we all cry in unison.

I look back towards the shed, half expecting to see the television miraculously gone, but it's obvious from the large, black shape jutting awkwardly out of the earth that, thankfully, this is not the case.

'The winners! The winners!' Dr Krapotkin hoots, pointing wildly in our direction. 'That's 2–1 if I'm not mistaken. And if we win the next one, we'll have to go to a tie-breaker.'

'**If**,' scoffs Sir Sting-A-Lot. 'And that's a very big **if**.'

'Oh, do pipe down, you old windbag,' Dr Krapotkin retorts, gleefully pulling out the next challenge. 'Next up – an oldie, but a goodie. Challenge four, HIDE AND WE COME SEEK. Let's see how good you pesties are at hiding. Last creature to be found wins and so too does their team. You have twenty seconds, starting now. TWENTY ...!'

She and Sir Sting-A-Lot cover their eyes and begin to count.

With a stampeding of feet, everyone is gone before she gets to 'nineteen'.

This is perfect. I'm great at hiding. I pick a direction and run, confident I will find something I can tuck myself in, or under. I've gone about one hundred paces when I come across an old, leathery glove hidden in amongst the grass. I wiggle underneath it and immediately hit something warm and furry.

'Watch it, house mouse. This is my spot. Go and find your own,' sighs Winx, who appears to be using the game as an excuse to have a lie down.

'Oh ... er, I'm sorry ... terribly sorry,' I say, quickly backing out.

'15 ... 14 ... 13 ...' counts Dr Krapotkin.

What am I doing? Why I am being so stupidly polite? I need to be cool. A cool mouse would have said, 'Hey, don't be so rude!' which would have been much more appropriate.

'12 ... 11 ... 10 ...'

Out of the corner of my eye I glimpse Sly. 'See ya, loser,' he says, disappearing up the tall green stalk of a nearby plant.

'9 ... 8 ... 7 ...'

From under the glove I hear Winx giggle.

'6 ... 5 ...'

I spot a large stone; I try to get underneath it, but it's too heavy, so I make do with pressing myself against it. I'm grey, the rock is grey, it's dark ... I cross my fingers and all my toes.

'Ready or not, here we come,' calls Dr Krapotkin.

In what feels like a nano-second, I hear the buzz of wings. 'Found the mouse!' Sir Sting-A-Lot buzzes gleefully.

My heart sinks. I can't believe it. Me, a hiding expert, the first to be found.

'Found the squirrels,' I hear Dr Krapotkin cry cheerily from across the garden.

I make my way back to the garden shed and wait as, one by one, everyone else is found. Finally, there are just two left hiding: Winx and Underlay.

I curse myself for not finding the leather glove first.

'If Underlay doesn't win this challenge,' whispers Dug nervously, 'it's all over.'

We watch in silence as Dr Krapotkin and Sir Sting-A-Lot circle the garden. Dr Krapotkin glides past the glove.

'Stop!' I want to cry. 'Look under it.' If only there was a way I could secretly signal to her.

Sir Sting-A-Lot is fast; he zips this way and that, frantically checking for a sign of Underlay. 'I'm going to find you, little pest,' he calls out. 'Any minute now ...'

Dr Krapotkin turns and circles back towards the glove. 'Come on, come on,' I mutter, clenching and unclenching my paws nervously. My heart sinks as she passes above it again, but then ... she tilts her head to one side ... she's heard something. Her body slows, and she turns back. Yes! Yes! Down she swoops, on to the glove, grabbing it in her claws and lifting it up.

'The mouse, the mouse,' she whoops. 'I've found the mouse.'

'Wooo-hooo,' I cry, unable to hold in my relief.

'Get in there!' Dug yells, pumping his large fist.

V.E.R.M.I.N. look over and jeer. But I don't care — we've won! We've pulled it back to 2–2. I can't believe it.

Underlay appears from the left leg of a pair of pants on the washing line. From the look of them, they've been hanging there a very long time.

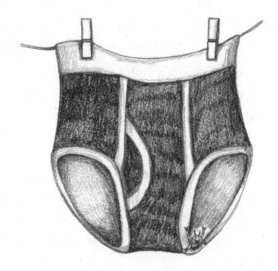

'Hooray!'veNeverWonAnythingBefore,' she cheers, clapping her front claws.

We all cheer too, Dr Krapotkin loudest of all. 'It's a tie-

breaker, a tie-breaker,' she sings at the top of her voice. 'We're going to a tie-breaker! We're gonna win!'

I look over at V.E.R.M.I.N. Everything about them says there is no way they are going to let us take the victory. I glance at Winx, still haunted by my over-polite apology. She yawns and rolls her eyes. I quickly look away, pretending to be brushing something off the bottom of my foot.

For the final time, Sir Sting-A-Lot disappears into the

plant pot. 'WHEELIE WRECKER,' he reads. 'First to tip over a wheelie bin wins. On your marks, get set ...'

V.E.R.M.I.N. are off before he gets to 'go'. But there's no time to protest.

'I've got Underlay,' says Batz.

'I've got Webbo,' calls back Maximus.

And with that we sprint as fast as we can back to the mansion block and the two huge, black plastic bins that stand to one side of it.

'Quick,' I hear Ronnie call out, as I see the lid of one of them fly open. 'Lighten the load.' Both squirrels dive in and, before we've even reached the bins, black bags of rubbish start flying up into the air.

And that's when a faint but unmistakable scent hits my nose. It stops me dead in my tracks. I sniff again, trying to tune out the smell of rotting rubbish. There it is ... a faint tang of wood, smoke and ...

Images of Tarquin's flat, of the sofa, of Batz pointing at it and saying 'that's where SHE sleeps,' flash through my mind.

'Death,' I gasp. 'I smell—'

'—cats!' cries Winx. Of course, she's smelt it too. 'They're close ...!'

'Not just close,' purrs an eerily soft voice, as out of the shadows slink three terrifying shapes, 'but **all** around you.'

# BATZ, BIN BAGS AND BADNESS

Fear rips through my body like nothing I've felt before. My fur stands on end like it's trying to leave my body and run away. Every one of my senses is going crazy. I'm caught between the urge to curl myself into a ball, and

90

the urge to flee. But if I were to run there would be no point – the cats have us surrounded.

'The Mogg,' Dug whimpers.

'I thought they never visit the garden,' I whisper back.

'They don't,' he replies. 'They shouldn't be here.'

A large white cat slouches towards us. 'OK, my lovelies. Now, stay calm and no one gets hurt,' she purrs coolly.

'Fluffy,' snarls Dr Krapotkin, who has landed beside us. 'The Husband Slayer.'

Big Bob

Fluffy

Fluffy grins and licks her lips. 'Indeed, it is me, and this is my gang.' She sweeps a paw at the other two cats. 'Big Bob and Kitten Cat. And you **will** do as we say, because if

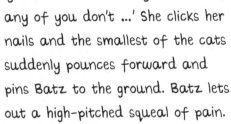

any of you don't ...' She clicks her nails and the smallest of the cats suddenly pounces forward and pins Batz to the ground. Batz lets out a high-pitched squeal of pain.

'... Kitten Cat will eat the bat ... Hey, that rhymes! Kitten Cat will eat the bat ... See what I did there?'

Batz yelps as Kitten Cat hooks a claw into one of her wings and drags her backwards.

'Stop, you're hurting her!' I blurt, rushing forward, but I've only taken two steps when THWACK! Something hits me hard, knocking me off my feet.

'Like I said, keep calm and no one gets hurt,' says Fluffy, dusting off her paw. I pull myself to my feet, rubbing my head. 'OK, Mogg, commence the herding,' she commands, and the cats take another step forward, forcing us all to bunch up tighter.

'It's OK, darlinks. It's going to be OK,' Dr Krapotkin whispers, but I can tell from the tone of her voice she's just as frightened as we are.

'There's gotta be some way out of this mess,' Winx hisses.

'Yes, please do something,' Dug whimpers.

'Button it, or Kitten Cat gets an early breakfast,' Fluffy snarls.

Kitten Cat does something that makes Batz cry out again. The sound of my best friend in pain makes me feel sick. Next to me I feel Dug shudder and look over just in time to see a tear tumble down his furry cheek. Ronnie and Reggie's tails are twitching even more madly than Fluffy's, and Sly has disappeared so far into his shell it's impossible to tell if he's still in there.

Big Bob lumbers forward. Carefully, using his claws, he undoes the knot on one of the less full bags of rubbish that Ronnie and Reggie just threw out of the bin.

'Now, if you would all be kind enough to hop in the sack, we can conclude this meeting,' says Fluffy, merrily.

'Get into a sack full of stinking garbage?!' Dr Krapotkin squawks.

'No, into a warm bath of bubbles,' replies Fluffy, sarcastically. 'Yes, in the sack and hurry up, we're on a deadline.'

Big Bob circles back around and starts nudging us forward. I feel his warm, death-tinged breath tickling my fur. I hear Kitten Cat giggle and then Batz lets out another yelp.

'So, you're putting us in the garbage sack and then what?' asks Sir Sting-A-Lot as we shuffle into the gaping mouth of the foul-smelling bag. It's like the rubbish has made the air thicker somehow — when I breathe in, it's like inhaling a soup made solely of stench.

'Yes, I don't get it. Why don't you want to eat us?' adds Dr Krapotkin, her foot squelching into something black and gooey.

'We're saving ourselves for something much tastier,' Fluffy grins. 'We've got Mega Meaty Kitty Treaties, the tastiest treaties in the world, waiting for us.'

'Who has promised you these? And why?' hoots a puzzled Dr Krapotkin.

'Stop all this chitter-chatter and GET IN THE SACK.'

Fluffy ignores her question. 'We need to get back to the basement to collect them before it's too late. Don't want the treaties to go up in smoke as well.' She addresses this last line to the other cats, who immediately look concerned.

Big Bob shoves us roughly forward.

'UP IN SMOKE? WHAT DO YOU MEAN?' squawks Dr Krapotkin. But her words are drowned out by our collective screams as Reggie and Ronnie lose their balance and tumble forward, knocking the rest of us into the putrid goo oozing from the sack.

'Batz!' I cry out, as I fall into a rotten orange. I don't want her thrown in here with us, but I can't bear the thought of what the Mogg might do with her out there.

'Aw, let me keep her,' I hear a babyish voice whine. 'She's my new favouwite play toy. Please, please, pretty please. You'd make Kitten Cat vewy happy.'

'Very well. But when you've finished, please make sure you eat her. I do so hate it when you leave dead bodies lying around,' Fluffy replies, curtly.

'No! No! Please, no!'

96

I cry out, slipping on a patch of slimy spaghetti and face-planting straight into Dug's furry bottom.

He reaches a large paw down and pulls me up. Around me my classmates and V.E.R.M.I.N. slither and slide further into the dark stinking gloom of the bin sack. 'WeCan'tLetThisHappen!' squeaks Underlay, but there's a line of snarling cats blocking our escape.

'Get off me!' I hear Batz cry. 'Stop, that hurts!'

We all let out another panicked scream as Big Bob reties the end of the bin bag and we are plunged into total, stinking, darkness.

# BINNED

All around me, my classmates and V.E.R.M.I.N. begin to panic and struggle. A large, furry foot thwacks me in the face, pushing my nose into the mush of a rotten banana. I feel the plastic of the sack pressing against my back. I scratch at it, trying to tear a hole, but it's too thick for my claws.

'I can't breathe, I can't breathe,' gasps Dug.

'Find something sharp,' squawks Dr Krapotkin. 'Something that we can rip our way out of the sack with.'

'Shirley ... you by any chance got a knife hidden in those pouches of yours?' shouts Winx.

But her question is met with silence.

'That little Houdini got away,' gasps Reggie.

My heart sinks. There **was** a way to escape. I curse myself for not seeing it as I blindly paw through the gooey gunk.

From outside we hear Fluffy's cruel laughter. 'Time to put them out of their misery. Mogg, commence the howl.'

All of a sudden, our ears are filled with a hideous, cacophonous yowling.

'What are they doing?' screeches Dr Krapotkin, fighting to make herself heard over the din. Then, just as suddenly as the howling starts, it stops, and for a second there is delicious silence.

And then ...

'Oi ... get away ... shoo ... shoo!' It's MyLove! I hear the slap, slap, slap of his slippered feet approaching the bin. 'For Pete's sake. You blimmin' cats. Tipping out the rubbish,' he curses. 'And now I've got to tidy up the mess.'

I feel my stomach lurch as we are lifted up. We all slide to one side, tumbling into each other. And then we slide to the other, and then we're falling and then BOMPH! We hit the bottom of the bin. And with another BOMPH!

BOMPH! BOMPH! the other bin bags rain down on top of us, pressing us all deeper into the stinking rubbish.

In the distance, my ears pick up the roar of a large engine.

'Thank goodness.' I hear MyLove sigh wearily. 'Here come the bin men.'

'Oh, no, oh, no, the bin lorry! We're going to be chomped up and squished flat,' Dug cries, his body pushing me further into the goo of a mouldy tomato. 'Help! Help!'

'Oi, mole, get your stupid, fat paw out of my face,' Ronnie snaps.

'Hey! Don't talk about him like that,' I shout back.

'Or you're going to do what about it?' sneers Reggie.

'We'll all do something about it,' snarls Maximus. 'If we hadn't had to go into your stupid garden for stupid Sports Night, then we wouldn't be in this mess.'

'Well, if your stupid bat friend hadn't got herself held hostage, we might have had a chance of getting away,' Winx retorts.

'Children, children, that is quite enough!' squawks Dr Krapotkin. 'We are all in this stinking mess together. Come on, we need to work collaboratively ... power in numbers.' I catch a hint of desperation in her voice. 'Scratch and claw, rip and tear — we have to get out of here.'

Her words clearly make an impression as all around me biting and slashing erupts. In the darkness it's impossible to tell who, or what, is where. I push my way through the soft gunk of the tomato, then claw my way through the crunchy jumble of some eggshells. But I can't tell which way is up and which is down. I feel a sob of despair rise in my throat.

'This isn't going to work,' sighs a deflated-sounding Sir Sting-A-Lot. 'Even if we get out of this sack, there are another four above us.'

From outside there comes another mighty roar: the bin lorry. It's hardly any distance from us at all. Around me my classmates fall silent as the hopelessness of our situation sinks in.

'I want my mum,' I hear Dug sob. I half expect Dr Krapotkin to try to rally us one last time, but she too is silent.

From outside we hear MyLove. 'You done your business?

Good boy, Trevor. Now, let's get back to bed,' he says sleepily.

My heart skips a beat. 'Trevor!' I cry out. 'Trevor, is that you? Can you hear me?'

'Mouse?' he woofs.

'Yes, yes, we're in the bin,' I shout back with all my might.

'Where've I been?' he replies cheerily, clearly mis-hearing. 'I been having a wee. Thought might do a poo, but it not come.'

'Shush, Trevor, come on, you'll wake the neighbours,' I hear MyLove snap.

'NO! Not where've you been, WE'RE IN THE BIN,' I try desperately again.

'Mouse in bin?' laughs Trevor. 'What mouse do in there? Looking for cheese?'

The bin lorry comes to a skidding stop and I hear its door clunk open.

'We're trapped. We need you to help get us out!' I cry. 'Before it's too late.'

But it is too late. I hear the thud of heavy footsteps approaching.

'The bin men,' shouts Reggie. 'They're here!'

With a shudder our world suddenly tilts and we all slide to one side, into a stinking soup of scrambled egg and fishbones. I hear the sound of wheels rolling on gravel and then an unmistakable heavy, metallic clank, clank, clank!

'The crusher!' chorus Reggie and Ronnie in unison.

'TREEEEEEVOOOOR,' I scream. 'HELLLLP!'

Next to me Maximus starts to sob. An image of Grandma all tucked up safely in our nest pops into my head. Oh, Grandma, how I wish I was there with you right now.

'Hey ... what the ...?' shouts a gruff voice suddenly. With a loud BANG, something hits the side of the bin and I feel everything around me slide sideways, then with a thunderous CRASH! I am suddenly upside down.

'Get away, you miserable mutt,' the gruff voice curses. 'Darn dog knocking over the flippin' bin, what a mess. Oi, get out! Stop that ...'

    I hear ripping and tearing, then see light, and then ...

    'Mouse! Mouse!' woofs Trevor, his paws frantically digging at the black bags, pulling them out. 'You ok?'

    'Go, darlinks, go!' Dr Krapotkin cries.

    'You saved our lives!' I say to Trevor, as I haul myself out of the goo. 'You're amazing ... thank you ...' But my words are drowned out by the cry of the gruff-voiced mans. I look up and see him staring down at me.

'AHHHHHH!' he shrieks. 'A MOUSE! A MOUSE!' He stumbles backwards into the other mans behind him.

'There's two of them! And a pigeon and some squirrels and, oh my life ...! Get out, you filthy beasts, get out!' shrieks the other mans, stamping his huge feet towards us.

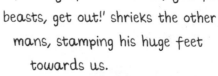

I turn and sprint as quickly as I can into the grass.

'Run, mouse, run!' barks Trevor.

I glance back over my shoulder just in time to see MyLove pulling him back into the block. 'Honestly, what has got into you?' He wags his finger in Trevor's face. 'Naughty, naughty boy!'

# V.E.S.T.S.

I reach the garden
shed just in time
to hear the bin
lorry pulling away.
All around me my
classmates tumble in,
stinky and covered
in rubbish. I have
porridge caked in my
ears and something
tomatoey smeared all
down one side.

'Please, err, don't tell anyone about the crying,' whispers Maximus. 'I mean, it wasn't fear ... it, um, it was some chopped onions I fell into.'

'Your secret's safe with me,' I say, zipping my mouth shut.

'Well, that was an unbelievably close call ... but all credit to Rover for helping us out.' A bedraggled-looking Dr Krapotkin, a lump of something green dripping off one of her wings, limps in. She opens her wings and Webbo and Underlay tumble out.

'ThanksMiss,' smiles Underlay, as she brushes a chunk of mouldy cookie off her shell.

I look around expecting to see my best friend, but she's not there.

'Batz!' I blurt. 'We have to save her.'

'And what did Fluffy mean when she said, "before the place goes up in smoke?" I'm no detective, but, dudes, something strange is clearly going down,' adds Webbo.

'Yes, yes, these are both most concerning issues,' says Dr Krapotkin, her head bobbing up and down vigorously. 'Ones we must hastily address.'

'And we would be happy to help you,' Sir Sting-A-Lot says, suddenly appearing next to her, a broad grin on his face.

'You would?' replies Dr Krapotkin, her eyebrows shooting off the top of her head.

'We may be bitter rivals, but that doesn't mean we are heartless ...'

He pauses. 'Well, I guess, being a wasp, I don't **technically** have a heart' – Sir Sting-A-Lot taps

his chest – 'but P.E.S.T.S. or V.E.R.M.I.N., we are the same. And that means that in adversity, we stick together!'

Dr Krapotkin looks genuinely shocked by this impromptu speech, but at the same time very pleased.

'Yes! Yes! V.E.R.M.I.N. and P.E.S.T.S. ... we could be

V.E.S.T.S.,' proclaims Dug, rather over-enthusiastically. He looks at us, clearly pleased with his suggestion. 'And on the other paw, maybe not,' he mutters, as his idea fails to get a response.

'OK, darlinks, we have two challenges. Number one, rescue Batz from a notorious group of murdering cats. Number two, find out who's supplying them with the treaties and what exactly that creature is up to.' She looks around at us all. 'It's time to get back to the basement!'

'Whoop! Let's go!' says Winx, her voice flat and sleepy. If she really is excited, she sure doesn't sound it.

'I'll set my nose to **Constant Sniff Mode**,' I add. Winx turns and looks at me, drowsily. I start to feel foolish again. 'Just in case, you know, the Mogg aren't **all** in the basement,' I clarify.

I know it's silly, but something about her cool way of being makes me want to impress her.

'Good thinking,' she nods after an agonisingly long pause. 'Didn't know you house mice knew about that kind of thing.'

I'm not sure if I should take this as a compliment or not. But I am pleased that she thought my suggestion was good.

'You know, it could get pretty gnarly in there,' she continues, as we all make our way back across the garden. 'There're no guarantees we're all going to make it out alive.'

'I don't care,' I reply. 'My friend is in danger. I'll do whatever I can to try and save her.'

'You really are a whole big sack of surprises,' she says. 'Maybe I got you wrong.'

'Maybe you did,' I say, mimicking her sleepy style.

She smiles back.

The stench of cat coming from the basement's air vent is unbelievably strong: there is no doubt the Mogg are inside. I feel all the hair on my body stand on end; I look across at Winx and see it's had the same effect on her. We both look like fur balls.

'We need a plan!' Sir Sting-A-Lot buzzes, nervously zipping back and forth.

'No time for that,' answers Dr Krapotkin, briskly. 'Batz could be Kitten Cat's snack at any moment. We've no option but to go in, get boots on the ground, assess the lie of the land – we're going to need to think on our feet.'

'Good to see you haven't forgotten our days in the military, Lieutenant,' replies Sir Sting-A-Lot, saluting her abruptly.

'Indeed, this old battle bird has not, Sergeant Major,' she replies, saluting back.

My classmates and I swap looks of surprised confusion. What kind of crazy history have these two shared?

'Well, come on, what are we waiting for?' Reggie pushes forward and squeezes himself through the grate. 'We've not got all night.'

All my senses are telling me this is a bad, bad idea. But I know I have to go in. I clench my paws, take four deep breaths and carefully follow my classmates and V.E.R.M.I.N. into the basement.

As I make my way down the old ladder I glance out across the room. In the inky darkness I can just make out the wardrobe, and the shadowy figures of the Mogg, circling what looks to be a large mountain of dirt. I can't see Batz, though.

**Maybe she's not here, maybe Kitten Cat has eaten her already.** My stomach lurches at the thought.

'Psst. Soldiers. Over here,' whispers Dr Krapotkin, waving furiously for us to join her behind the box of records. 'We need to get up close and personal — find out what's going down. Our secret weapon here is stealth ... so, let's move closer. ZERO noise.'

We all silently nod our agreement.

'On my command, this way.' She points towards the stack of paint tins, and we all fall into line behind her, following as quietly and as carefully as we can. Even

Maximus, normally so heavy on his feet, is on the tips of his toes.

The smell of cat gets stronger with every step; it takes every ounce of my strength not to turn and run away.

We reach the tins and Dr Krapotkin motions for us to huddle in behind them and listen. It's amazing I can hear anything over the frantic beating of my heart.

Fluffy is talking and she's clearly not happy. 'The deal was ten Mega Meaty Kitty Treaties to dispose of the pesty creatures, and ten to move the bat poop from the garden to here,' she snarls angrily.

For a moment there is silence, then, from the direction of the wardrobe comes a soft, **tick-tack, click-clack.**

It sounds like the snapping of claws.

We all look at one another – what could it be?

Tick-tack, click-clack, the noise comes again.

'Well ... come on ...' snaps Fluffy. 'Say something!'

I'm dying to peek to see who she is talking to. We all are. Dr Krapotkin motions furiously for us to stay still.

After what seems like for ever, the creature clears its throat. 'You are one hundred per cent sure they're **all** dead?'

Dr Krapotkin's eyes bulge so wide I worry they might pop.

'No!' mutters Dug. 'Please. Surely, it can't be.'

We all glance nervously at one another. It's impossible – we squashed him flat, with Tarquin's enormous nutty poo. The C.O.P.s (Council of Pests) came and took him away. They locked him up in prison. How can he be back?

'Crushed flat as pancakes, like I requested?' he continues, probing the Mogg for an answer.

'Sweet buzzards on high,' whimpers Dr Krapotkin. 'The monster is back.'

# RETURN OF THE 'ROACH

'Is that him?' whispers Sir Sting-A-Lot, a look of terror in his eyes. 'The cockroach who tried to blow up the block?'

He looks to Dr Krapotkin for an answer, but she's gone into some kind of panicked trance. 'I won't let him trick me and lock me in a suitcase again; no, I won't, I won't,' she mutters furiously under her breath, her head bobbing wildly up and down.

'He sounds just like the thieving cockroach we collected all that bat poop for,' whispers Ronnie.

No way! **They** were the creatures bothering Batz and her relatives.

'We nicked a phone for him too,' replies Reggie. 'He promised nuts, only he never paid up.'

'And whose fault was that?' snaps Ronnie, her tail starting to flick.

Sir Sting-A-Lot shoots them a stern look, but neither of them takes any notice.

'Well, you were the one who did the deal ...' snarls

Reggie, his tail now flicking wildly too.

'Will you please both—' snaps Sir Sting-A-Lot, but it's too late. Ronnie's tail hits one of the tins of paint. It wobbles one way, then the other, and then with a crash it falls, taking three more with it. Reggie stumbles forward and all the rest go flying.

'WHAT IN THE NAME OF SALMONELLA ...?' blusters Professor Armageddon, staring down at us, his antennae waggling madly on top of his head. 'You are supposed to be DEAD, kaput, gone! This was my glorious revenge! You squashed me, I crush you! Yet here you are, still very much three-dimensional! Would someone like to elaborate ...?'

He glares down at the Mogg, letting out a long, loud hiss. Fluffy looks back sheepishly.

Under Kitten Cat's left paw I see the tattered shape of Batz. She lifts a limp wing and attempts a wave. She's alive!!!

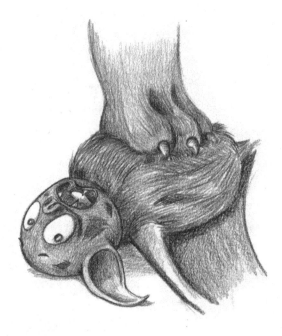

'Hide, darlinks, hide!' Dr Krapotkin squawks, snapping out of her daze. 'Don't listen to a word Professor Armageddon says! He'll only convince you to do something terrible.'

'Oi, Professor Arma-do-daa, we want our nuts! We

worked hard to get all that poo for you,' shouts Ronnie, pointing at the pile in the middle of the room, clearly unbothered by Dr Krapotkin's warning.

'And why's it in here? We left it in the garden!' chips in Reggie.

'And what's all this doo-doo for, anyway?' Professor Armageddon laughs mockingly. 'Well, let me educate your tiny brains. You see bat poo, or **guano**, to give it its technical name, is high in something called potassium nitrate — oh, the things you learn when your prison is in an old library ... thanks for helping me escape by the way ... being flat made slipping through the bars so easy.' He lets out a little chortle. 'Anyway, as I was saying, long ago the mans learnt how to use it and you know what they turned it into?' He looks down at us, daring us to know the answer to his question. 'The mans turned it into ... gunpowder. And you know what you can do with gunpowder, don't you?'

Dug raises a shaky paw, 'You're not going to attempt to blow up the block again?'

'Bravo! Top marks to the mole.' The professor claps. 'Though I do find the use of the word "attempt" rather

offensive. I AM going to blow up the block, you dozy dirt-digger. KABOOM, it's going to go up like a firework.' His antennae stand to excited attention. 'See that wire ...?' He points to a length of thin, silver cable protruding from the poo. 'It's hooked up to a detonator, and when I key in the special code, BOOM!' he mouths, throwing all his arms out wide. 'And this time you are NOT going to stop me because I've got' – he takes three lumps of something from a bag next to him – 'protection. Though, to be clear, I'm NOT paying them for the services they DID NOT manage to perform.'

He tosses the lumps at Fluffy.

'TEN treaties for carrying the poop. We might not have killed the pests, but you are blowing up the block. You're making us homeless,' she growls. 'Only Mega Meaty Kitty Treaties will soothe that pain.'

'Well now, about that.' Professor Armageddon shrugs, casually kicking away what is clearly a now-empty bag.

The Mogg emit a collective, angry snarl. 'We're hungry, very hungry,' Fluffy growls. 'We only had a light supper, because **you** promised treaties. Lots of them.'

Batz lets out a pained howl. I turn and see Kitten Cat retract a long, sharp claw back into her paw. What has she just done?!

'Well, then, why don't you ... eat the bat?' suggests Professor Armageddon.

'No! Please, you can't,' I shout, unable to stop myself.

'A bat is **not** sufficient fodder for three ravenous cats,' Fluffy snarls.

'So why don't you do yourselves and me a favour and have a buffet,' replies the professor gleefully, sweeping an arm in our direction. 'Here we have assembled a veritable cornucopia of delights: a brace of mice, a rat, a couple of squirrels, a plump-ish pigeon ... honestly, you won't need to eat for days after a blow-out like that! It's not quite the revenge I had planned for them, but they'll still all die ... painfully. And this way I get a grandstand view.'

The Mogg heads all swivel as one in our direction and, as if to prove just how hungry they are, Big Bob's stomach lets out a thunderous rumble.

'It's not what we agreed, but I suppose needs must,' says Fluffy, her eyes narrowing.

Next to me I feel Maximus tremble. 'Oh, we're in big trouble now,' he whimpers. 'We're definitely going to die this time.'

# SURELY NOT SHIRLEY!

With a sudden flurry of fur and claws, the basement descends into chaos.

'Distract, delay and get away!' Sir Sting-A-Lot cries as the Mogg pounce. Around me everyone scatters. Quick as a flash, I dive behind a stack of magazines.

'RUN, DARLINKS! RUN! I'LL HOLD THEM OFF FOR AS LONG AS I CAN,' I hear Dr Krapotkin squawk over the sound of her flapping wings. Ronnie and Reggie bound past me and scamper up the grandfather clock. 'You may have eaten my husband, but I won't let you lay a claw on my pupils!'

123

Dr Krapotkin screeches.

I look over at Kitten Cat. 'Mummy said you should always play with your food,' she says, nudging Batz's limp body back and forth with her paw.

Behind me I hear the crash of boxes. 'Don't think you can hide from me, mole!' I hear Fluffy laugh.

'Leave him alonezzzzz!' buzzes a frantic-sounding Blue.

'But playtime's over now.' Kitten Cat runs her tongue over her sharp, pointy little teeth. 'Now it's time for dinner.'

'No!' I scream, breaking cover. 'Eat me! Come on, catch me if you can!' It's the only thing I can think to do. Batz has no chance against her, but me, maybe ... Kitten Cat looks up and smiles – I've got her attention. 'Mice are far tastier than bats,' I continue, turning to run. But then ...

BOMPH!

One moment I'm standing, the next I'm flat on my back; a heavy, furry weight pressing me into the floor.

'Got a mouse.' It's Big Bob. He holds me down with his large paw.

'Stix!' Batz cries out weakly. I look across and see her clearly now. Her nose is smeared with blood and one of her wings is torn; she looks awful.

'I've got the rest of them trapped in the corner,' Fluffy gloats.

From the other end of the room I hear the crash of falling objects. I try to wriggle free from Big Bob's grasp, but he's far too strong. 'Not quite all of them!' I hear Ronnie shout. I look up just in time to see her flying towards us, fists outstretched. But Big Bob sees her too and neatly steps to the side. Ronnie slams into the leg of the wardrobe, knocking herself unconscious.

'Now I got a squirrel too,' he cheers.

'Nooooo,' Dr Krapotkin screeches.

'Excellent!' Professor Armageddon claps. 'And please ... be sure you finish the job this time!'

Maximus was right, we are all going to die. What were we thinking, taking on a gang of cats?

'Shall I eat you head to tail, or tail to head?' Big Bob grins down at me with hungry eyes.

'How about you don't eat 'im at all!'

'Shirley?' cries Winx. 'Shirley, is that you?'

Surely it can't be? He ran away – why on earth would he want to come back?

'Sure is, sweet cheeks,' he replies.

I twist my head around, trying to locate him.

He's standing, pouches full to bursting, on top of the bookcase. 'Did ya really fink I'd leave ya all hung out to dry? Nah ... I went

back to the pet shop.' His eyes sparkle with excitement. 'Knew they had just what was needed to sort the situation.'

'A hamster!' Kitten Cat giggles. 'I've always wanted a pet hamster.'

'Sorry to let you down, sweetheart, but you ain't laying paws on me tonight.' Shirley reaches into his bulging pouches and scoops out three plastic bags. He slashes them open with his claws, pulling out tiny balls of what appears to be some kind of herb and tossing them at the cats. 'You ain't gonna be laying paws on much when you get a snifter of what your boy Shirl's gone and got ya.'

One of the balls falls near us and I feel Big Bob's grip suddenly soften. Something warm and wet drops on my head, and I look up to see a line of drool dribbling from one side of his open mouth.

'**Nepeta cataria**,' I hear Dug gasp, from the other side of the basement. I've no idea what he means, but Big Bob does.

'Cat nip,' he mutters, more drool spilling out. 'Cat nip.'

'Cat nip, cat nip, cat nip!' the Mogg all begin to chorus as if in some kind of trance.

'Sure is,' Shirley yells, tossing yet more balls of it this way and that. 'Tuck in, SUCKERS!'

# ARMY-GEDDON

The Mogg dive around the basement,
each trying to find its own lump
of catnip. Fluffy launches
herself on to a ball of some,
grabbing it between her front
paws and rubbing it over her
body.

'You useless fat lumps
of fur!' cries Professor
Armageddon. 'Can't
you do anything
right?!'

129

'No,' giggles Big Bob, releasing me from his grasp and bounding over to a lump. He throws himself on top of it and begins rolling around in complete ecstasy.

'All right, listen in,' says Shirley. 'We ain't got much time – stuff's gonna wear off after a couple of minutes. We need to get outta here, and quick.'

'Batz!' I cry, rushing over to her limp body. Kitten Cat is now too busy nuzzling a lump of catnip by the wardrobe to notice or care.

Reggie bounds over and shakes Ronnie back to her senses.

'Batz, are you OK? Can you move?' I peer down at her poor battered body. Behind me I hear Dr Krapotkin desperately trying to gather everyone.

Dug whimpers that his foot has been bitten and I hear Winx rushing to help.

'It's just my wing, but it'll heal.' She tries to pull herself up. 'Ooof – and my ribs.' She winces.

Above me I pick up the distinct sound of insect legs scrabbling on wood, and I look up just in time to see Professor Armageddon scuttling away.

'He's gone to get the detonator,' winces Batz. 'You need to cut the wire.'

'Go ahead,' sneers Professor Armageddon, as he disappears into a pile of clutter. 'It makes no difference to me ...' And that's when I see it. The wire branches off into five, six, maybe as many as ten other wires, each of them disappearing into the ceiling above us. There must be more guano hidden up there. The whole place is rigged to explode!

'You need to go ... chase after him ... stop him,' Batz says, croakily. 'My family is in the roof, yours is in Flat 3. We can't let him do this.'

'But what about you?' I say. 'I can't just leave you here like this. I've got to get you out.'

'I'll get her out.' I spin around to see Maximus. He has another tear in his ear and a long scratch down the side of his cheek. 'You go after the professor. I'll make sure she gets out OK.' He offers her his paw.

I'm so stunned that I'm momentarily lost for words. Did he really just offer to do something thoughtful and nice?

'We're a team, remember? We look out for each other. Now, GO!' he says. 'Before I change my mind.'

In the far corner Dr Krapotkin and Sir Sting-A-Lot are herding my wounded friends towards the old ladder. I see Winx propping up a limping Dug, and Reggie helping a still very dazed Ronnie.

I'm the only one who has seen the professor escaping; I'm the only one in a position to stop him doing this terrible thing. 'You can do this, Stix,' I mutter under my breath. 'It's do, or everyone dies.'

Out of the corner of my eye I glimpse him dart up the wall and disappear through a tiny gap in the bricks. I bound as fast as I can across the room, leaping from box to box. I reach the wall and, using the small cracks in the brickwork and rough lumps to help me, I begin to climb.

Fast as I can, I scramble up. The hole the professor

squeezed himself through is tiny, but if there is one thing we mice are good at, it's getting through small gaps. I force my head into the crevice, then wiggle my shoulder blades together and slide the rest of my body in. I scrape and claw my way through, and finally tumble out the other side.

I hit the ground and scramble to my feet. I hear the leaves of a nearby bush rattle and run over just in time to see Professor Armageddon's shiny cockroach bottom disappear into them. He's climbing up the bush and he's fast. I dive in and follow.

I've climbed up chair legs before, but this is different – it's much more twisty – and the higher I climb, the denser the leaves of the plant become. Ahead, I can see them stretching right up the side of the block. I'm soon exhausted. I stop momentarily to catch my breath, gulping in deep lungfuls of cool night air.

'You'll not stop me this time, mouse!' I hear the professor cackle. 'No one will stop me this time.'

'Want to bet?' I wheeze, diving back into the leaves.

Finally, they begin to clear and I see the sky. Its faint

pinkish tinge tells me that dawn is fast approaching.

Ahead of me I see Professor Armageddon's back legs disappear over the lip of the gutter at the top of the building. I grit my teeth and scramble after him. But the plant's branches become thinner and thinner, making it harder to cling on to. I try not to look down, but I can't help myself. Arghhh, I'm so high up – one missed hand hold and I'm a goner. My palms start to sweat; my heart feels like a small fist trying to escape my chest. Images of the time I fell from Colin's window flash through my mind.

**Focus!** I tell myself, tearing my eyes away from the distant ground beneath me. 'Come on, Stix, FOCUS.'

The final, thin branch of the plant reaches the gutter and stops. I cling to it, gripping tightly with my back paws whilst reaching up with my front ones, fumbling for the gutter's lip. I grab hold of it then, using the last of my strength, haul myself up and over the slippery, plastic surface.

I'm exhausted – every muscle in my body is begging me to lie down and rest.

But I can't. I mustn't. I hear the clitter-clatter of Professor Armageddon's claws scrambling up the tiles of the roof. I pull myself out of the gutter and up after him.

The roof is MASSIVE. It stretches out in front of me like a steep, black mountain. Dotted across its surface are green, hairy lumps of moss.

'Hey!' I shout after him. 'Stop! You can't do this.'

'Oh, but I can,' he grins, glancing over his shoulder. 'I'm Professor Armageddon. The clue is in the name.' He reaches a large, white plastic object and stops.

What is that thing? It looks like ... **No. It can't be.** 'Is that ... is that Boo-Boo's phone?'

'If you mean, is this the toy phone of the disgusting mans child that lives in Flat 3, then yes, it is. I got those numbskull squirrels to steal it.' He cackles gleefully, leaping up on to it. 'And if you take one step closer, I'll start typing in the detonation code.' He points down at the phone's large, colourful buttons and then to the thin wire that runs all the way down the roof and back into the building. 'Hard-wired into the fuse in the middle of all that lovely, highly explosive guano. When I type the correct combination into the phone, it will trigger the charge and BOOM! It's party time! Well, not for the mans who are still sleeping in their beds – they'll never know what hit them. It's going to be the ultimate act of pestilence and I'm going to go down in history! Tell me, mouse, who's got the deadly poo **this** time? Ha, ha, ha!'

I think of little Boo-Boo tucked up in her cot, Grandma curled up in our nest, Trevor snoring on his dog bed – all oblivious to what this crazy cockroach is about to do. 'Well,' I say, 'it's one against one. Me against you.' I leap towards him. A few more bounds and I will be able to get to him and knock him off the phone. 'I'll stop you before you get a chance to key in the—'

'ARMY,' commands Professor Armageddon. 'RISE.' He lifts his arms and, with a creaking groan, all the tiles around me lift. Out spills cockroach after cockroach after cockroach. They teem out in their hordes until a wall of

them stands in front of me, blocking my path. They stare at me, clacking their pincers. Click, clack, click, clack.

'The connections you make in prison can get you anything you need ... even an army of 'roaches,' the professor laughs, his beady eyes gleaming with delight. 'Brought them as backup, just in case the C.O.P.S. caught up with me faster than expected. They'll have no problem protecting me from a snivelling little mouse.'

'Ha! Ha! Ha!' laugh the cockroaches in unison.

'Not just a snivelling little mouse!' At the sound of her voice, I spin around to see a tattered Batz hauling herself up the roof towards me. 'But his best friend too.'

'Not the blasted bat as well,' Professor Armageddon growls, rolling his eyes.

'And ... the ... rat,' pants an exhausted Maximus, pulling himself over the rim of the gutter and promptly collapsing on the roof.

'I got him to carry me up here,' Batz grins. 'Couldn't let you deal with the nutty professor all on your own.'

'Well, we've got a lot of problems,' I reply, smiling back at her.

'Yup,' she nods as the mass of cockroaches all take a step towards us. 'We sure do.'

# STICK!

I look at Batz, at her wounded wing, at her battered face. What an amazing friend she is. And Maximus too. No wonder he's exhausted – I wouldn't be able to carry Batz more than a couple of paces, let alone all the way up the side of a building.

The cockroaches let out a loud hiss and, as one, they take another step forward, forcing me and Batz to step back.

'They're going to drive us off the roof,' she says, panic creeping into her voice. 'And you can't fly and, at the moment, neither can I.'

'What an observant bat you are,' the professor beams.

'Roaches, faster.'

**STOMP! STOMP! STOMP!** The cockroaches speed up.

'Now all I have to do is type in the easy-to-remember, three-digit initiation code and tick-tock, it's **BOOM** o'clock. What was it again? Ah, yes, that's it ... two, four, six.' He gleefully jumps both feet down hard on the number two button.

'**Number two!**' sings Boo-Boo's phone. '**Two green bottles, sitting on the wall.**'

The cockroaches force us back yet further.

'**Two green bottles, sitting on the wall,**' sings the phone even more cheerfully.

'Ssh, ssh,' tuts the Professor. 'Why is it singing?'

'We've got to do something,' I say desperately, trying to stand my ground. I try to push back against the cockroaches, but their bodies are like iron, and though they are smaller than me, they are strong, very strong. There is no point trying to jump over them, either. There are just too many — they stretch back all the way to the professor.

'I've got an idea,' says Batz, tucking her wings tight to her body. 'I'll try and make you a path.' And with that she

launches herself forward into the wall. 'Strike!' she shouts as she knocks over a cockroach.

**'And if one green bottle, should accidentally fall ...'** chirps the phone.

I tuck myself in behind Batz, but for every cockroach she knocks over, another appears, taking its place.

'If only I could fly I'd be able to dive-bomb them,' she groans.

I glance back at Maximus. Maybe he could help?

'There'll be one green bottle, sitting on the wall,' concludes the phone.

'Thank goodness for that,' cries Professor Armageddon, neatly jumping both feet on number four.

'Argh!' cries Batz, as yet more cockroaches surge forward from under the roof tiles.

'We need your help!' I shout to Maximus. He's rummaging around in the gutter – what is he doing?!

'**Number four**,' announces the phone as a particularly large cockroach appears and smashes into Batz, knocking her back into me. I lose my footing and begin to slide backwards.

'**Four green bottles, sitting on the wall**,' sings the phone cheerily.

'No! No! Not again,' howls the professor, angrily.

I manage to grab hold of a large lump of moss and steady myself.

'SHUT UP! SHUT UP! STOP SINGING,' he bellows manically, stamping his foot on the phone to try and stop it.

'Argh, this is IMPOSSIBLE,' Batz cries, sliding back into me. We pick ourselves up, ready to try again, but we're running out of time ... and space. The cockroaches just keep on coming, hissing and clacking and driving us further and further from the professor – and closer to the edge of the roof.

'Give up, you're never going to get to me!' screams the professor, still desperately struggling to quiet the phone.

'Can't you see? You're going to be blown up too!' Batz replies, staggering backwards.

'Don't you remember anything? Nothing kills a cockroach, not even nuclear war,' he boasts, before adding, 'And we can live seven days without our heads. I'd like to see you try that!'

I look across at Batz. Her face mirrors the panic I feel. This is impossible. Oh, Grandma. Oh, Boo-Boo. Oh, Trevor. Oh, everyone in the block!

'Stick! Stick!' I hear Maximus shout. I spin around, furious that he should choose this moment to mock my name. Does he not care what is about to happen?

But he's not saying my name; he's holding up a long twig he's found in the gutter. 'Take it.' He tosses it towards me. 'Use it. You know how.'

'A stick ...?' the professor laughs. 'What are you going to do? Throw it at me? I've got a rock-hard exoskeleton; clearly you don't remember that either, fools!'

I look down at the stick in my hand, and then at the advancing sea of cockroaches. Maximus doesn't mean me to throw it, he means me to use it to vault over all of them ... but I'm not sure I've got what it takes.

'You can do it, Stix,' he says. 'I know you can.'

**'And if four green bottles, should accidentally fall ...'**

'He's right,' says Batz. 'You got this.'

Don't they recall my epic fail the other evening?

'Do it,' shouts Maximus. 'DO IT NOW!'

And with that I turn to face the 'roach army.

# LEAP OF FAITH

The cockroaches march forward once more. I have to act
before the space in front of me disappears completely.
I clutch the stick tightly in my front paws, grit my teeth,
slide a little further down the roof to give myself more
room, and then begin to run, as fast as I can.

The cockroaches immediately come to a stop and wrap
their wings around themselves; I guess they think I am
going to try and spear them. But I'm not, I'm about to try
something much more difficult.

I choose my spot and drive the stick as hard as I can

into a lump of moss. Using all my strength I propel my body up into the air. I feel the stick bend backwards, tilting me upside down. I kick my legs up. And, as the stick straightens, I feel, with a mighty whoosh, my body being propelled forward. It flings me violently over the cockroaches. I grip on as tightly as I possibly can – I am NOT letting go, not this time.

I look down and see the mass of them below me. I can't believe I've done it – I've finally managed a proper vault!

'FLY, STIX, FLY!' I hear Batz cheer as the cockroaches emit a loud hiss of surprise. The stick is straight. I've reached the highest point. As it begins to fall, so do I ...

'And now for the final number,' taunts Professor Armageddon, as the phone finally finishes singing. He lifts his foot and steps towards the number six.

I free my grip on the stick and, as I fall towards him, everything momentarily slows.

'Noooo,' I cry, as I watch him step one foot on the final button. 'Yes,' he grins, lifting his other foot. For a split second our eyes meet – his full of excitement, mine full of determination. Then, BAM! my body crashes into the phone.

The professor lets out an anguished cry and I look up to see him toppling towards me. He slams into me, pushing me on to the number eight. It sinks down as my bottom lands on it.

**'Number eight. Eight green bottles, sitting on the wall,'** sings the phone joyfully.

'NO!' screams the professor, as we both tumble off the phone on to the roof. 'No! No! NO! Now I have to start the sequence all over again!'

We both bounce down the roof, the phone somersaulting along behind us.

'I can't fail!

I won't fail!' he howls desperately, reaching for it. But the roof is steep, and our momentum increases with every tumble we take. He flaps around wildly, the phone crashing and bashing behind him, just out of his grasp.

**'And if eight green bottles, should accidentally fall ...'**

'Curse you, mouse!' he screams.

Whump! Thump! Bump! One second I'm looking at the black of the roof, next I'm looking at the grey of the sky. Over and over I somersault, like a pair of MyLove's pants on a spin cycle.

'STIX!' I hear Batz and Maximus cry out.

I might have stopped the professor detonating his bomb and blowing up the block, but there is no way I'm going to be able to stop myself tumbling off the edge of the roof. And there sure isn't going to be any Batz swooping down to save me this time.

Smack goes my head, bam goes my bottom. Splinters of thought whirl through my mind: Grandma holding out her arms to me, Boo-Boo's laughing, Trevor smiling, Batz giving me a high-five.

Then, with one stomach-churning final bounce, I feel my

body tumble out into thin air. I see the white, spinning shape of Boo-Boo's phone. It reaches the end of its wire and, with a violent jerk, it breaks free and tumbles over the edge of the roof. I follow after it, but there's nothing to stop me falling, limbs paddling wildly in the empty nothing.

But something is not right ...

... the ground isn't getting any closer ...

... I'm stuck in mid-air ...

... like time has suddenly ...

... inexplicably ...

... stopped.

# TAIL OF THE UNEXPECTED

But time hasn't stopped. Because beneath me I see Professor Armageddon still plummeting towards the ground, his wings frantically buzzing as he tries to slow his fall.

It's only me that's not moving. I feel a tug – something, or someone, is gripping the tip of my tail.

I turn my head trying to see who, or what, has just saved me.

A shadowy figure stares down at me. I blink, trying to make sense of the upside-down shape I am seeing. The creature pulls me back up on to the roof, and I realise I'm looking at a ... MOUSE! A tall, strong, grown-up mouse. In one paw he holds a long wooden stick, in the other he holds my tail. Gently he lowers me back on to the roof.

I hear a loud **thwack, thwack** and turn to see another mouse. She is nimbly somersaulting this way and that,

knocking the cockroaches off the roof with the stick in her hand. Crack, thwack, smack, she sends them flying up in the air. With one final strike she dispenses with the last of them, then plants her stick in front of her and neatly uses it to vault to where the male mouse and I are standing.

'Woah!' I hear Maximus and Batz both say in unison.

The lady mouse peers over the edge of the roof. 'Ah, good, Ash has him restrained,' she says, turning back to us.

I peek over and see another mouse, even bigger than the two I am with, sitting on top of the professor, pinning him to the ground.

'Y—You're amazing … who are you?' I stammer.

Both mice look at one another and then back at me. 'We are somebody and we are nobody,' says the lady mouse mysteriously, taking my paw in hers.

'We're from S.M.A.R.T. The Secret Mouse Aerial Response Troop. We were deployed to capture the escaped roach,' the male mouse tries to explain, clearly sensing my confusion at his friend's answer.

'And you were a huge help, Stix. That was some vault,' says the lady mouse.

'You know my name?'

'We know ever so much about you.' She squeezes my paw tightly.

'Indeed, we do,' says the other mouse, ruffling the fur on the top of my head.

'Do you know about me too?' says Maximus, eagerly bounding over. 'I helped as well! I gave him the stick.'

'A Raticus,' says the lady mouse, eyeing Maximus suspiciously.

'I'm his friend!' declares Maximus. He looks at me and beams.

'Er, yeah, he is,' I say,

smiling back, not quite sure what to think about any of this.

'Well, we both knew you'd do well,' she says, turning her gaze back to me.

'You knew?' These mystery mice are more confusing by the minute. 'But how?'

'We both just did,' she smiles, giving my paw one final squeeze before letting go. For a moment I see sadness in her eyes, then with a shake of her head it's gone. 'Anyway, enough of all this. We've got a rogue roach to deal with,' she says. 'And, not a word of this to anyone. You never saw us, OK?'

We all nod as both mice take their sticks in their paws. 'Oh, I forgot,' the lady mouse says, turning back. 'Tell your grandma we said **hello**.'

'And ...' whispers the male mouse leaning forward so only I can hear, '... may the power of the mouse guide you.' He gives me a wink and then with a neat forward somersault, they both launch themselves off the roof.

All three of us rush to the edge and peer over, just in time to see them grab hold of the drainpipe and slide, with

well-practised skill, back down to the ground and scamper
away.

# AND THE WINNERS ARE ...

'What were you thinking? Telling them that the mouse is your friend?' Plague One sneers as we make our way back across the roof.

'Yeah, have you lost your teeny-tiny mind?' chips in Plague Two. 'You hate mice.'

'Maybe I've had a change of heart ...' Maximus snarls angrily, swatting at them. 'I mean just a small one, nothing major.'

'Phew!' Batz laughs. 'Glad to hear you don't like him **too** much – we'd hate you to be completely reformed.'

'But perhaps we could start by trying to be more like friends than enemies,' I add hopefully. It would be so nice if he could stop being quite so horrible to me.

I've never had a friend,' Maximus shrugs. 'But, yes, I guess we could see how it goes.'

'But **we're** your friends,' Plague One protests. 'You don't need anyone but us.'

'I'd say you're more frenemies,' says Batz. 'You know, kind of good friends, kind of the worst, all at once.'

'We're frenemies,' Plague One sniggers.

'I like it,' Plague Two snorts.

'Well, now everyone's happy, how about a lift back down?' Batz says, smiling at Maximus. 'Pretty please ...'

His face drops. 'It was quite a struggle get you up,' he says, nervously. 'I'm not sure I've got the energy to-'

'Don't you worry. We got this.' It's Reggie. His head bobs up over the lip of the gutter, followed by Ronnie's. 'All aboard the bat bus,' she says, offering Batz her paw.


We get back to the shed to find everyone looking rather tatty and a bit beaten, but thankfully all fine. Winx is giving Dug a special herb she says will help his paw heal quicker, and Shirley is proudly handing out some seeds and nuts he also stole from the pet shop.

'Darlinks, darlinks, there you are!' Dr Krapotkin cries, flapping out of a rainwater-filled bucket she's been washing herself in. 'Whatever happened to you? We didn't know where you'd gone.'

'We got rid of Professor Armageddon, but I can't say any more than that,' says Maximus smugly. 'We've been sworn to secrecy by some secret creatures.' I can see he is very much enjoying the fact he knows something the rest don't.

'Ah, drat. You mean I missed out on the action,' Winx yawns, shaking her head.

'Well, it all sounds most amazing, darlinks,' says Dr Krapotkin, eyeing us suspiciously. 'I thought I caught sight of three grown-up mice just as we were getting everyone to safety. This wouldn't have anything to do with S.M.A.R.T., would it?'

'No way, absolutely nothing to do with them at all,' declares Maximus over-dramatically. 'I mean ... who are

S.M.A.R.T.? Never heard of them.'

I say nothing. I have a sneaking suspicion that Dr Krapotkin might know more than she is letting on.

Sir Sting-A-Lot seems more concerned about the outcome of our Sports Night than what we just got up to. For a moment I worry he is going to say we have to do it all over again.

'Now, if I may remind you, before we were rudely interrupted, first by the Mogg and then by that hideous cockroach fellow, we – P.E.S.T.S. and V.E.R.M.I.N. – had reached a draw.' He pauses, drawing in a long breath. 'However, in light of the final events of the evening, of whatever bravery the mouse, bat and rat just performed in order to avert what would have been quite a **catastrophic** incident – it gives me great pleasure to announce P.E.S.T.S. as this year's winners of the Mexico World Cup '86.'

I can tell from the pained look on his face it has not been easy for him to say this.

'Oh, darlinks! Oh, my darlinks!' Dr Krapotkin cries, jumping up and down excitedly. 'We did it. We did it. For the first time EVER the cup is ours.'

'OK, OK, don't overdo it or I might change my mind.' Sir Sing-A-Lot rolls his eyes.

'Group hug! Group hug!' continues Dr Krapotkin, throwing her wings open wide. We all bundle in and she wraps them tightly around us, squishing us all against her warm, feathery body.

'Oh, you've made this old pigeon so proud,' she coos.

'Aww, epic hug. Can we get one of those, sir?' pleads Winx, looking up at Sir Sting-A-Lot with big sleepy eyes.

'Er, well ... I'm not sure I've quite got the wingspan,' he replies, sounding a little embarrassed.

'Come in, darlinks, my wings are big enough

for ALL of you,' says Dr Krapotkin. And with that, I find myself in the biggest group hug I think it is possible to have.

The sun is well and truly up by now, so it's high time for us all to head back to our homes, and quickly.

Sir Sting-A-Lot promises he'll have Ronnie and Reggie come and clean out the bat poop from the basement; in the meantime, he commands them to help Batz back up to the roof and her family.

'Well, house mouse, I guess I'll see you around.' Winx gives me a friendly nudge.

'And, if you ever need someone to come get you out of a scrape' – Shirley winks – 'you know where your boy Shirl is.

By the way, I saved you this ...' He pulls a tiny shred of catnip from his pouch. 'Those cats should be tucked up back with their owners, but just in case they're not ...'

Sly declares himself 'not one for goodbyes'. But it's clear he is sad to see Underlay, Blue and Webbo go.

'It was nice for him to have creatures his own size,' whispers Winx.

By the time we get back to the basement I'm completely and utterly exhausted. I think that might just have been one of the longest nights of my life.

I bid good night to my classmates and wearily head over to the hidden highways. 'See ya later, alligator,' I wave to Maximus as he bounds towards the drain cover – the route back to his home in the sewers.

He pauses. For a moment I think he's about to slip back into his usual, nasty self and say something horrible. But instead he says, with a cheery smile: 'In a while, crocodile.'

# THE
# REVELATION

Surprisingly Grandma is still awake when I get back. 'There you are!' she says, throwing her arms around me. 'Ew, but

you smell bad.' She pulls back, her nose wrinkling. 'How was it? Did it all go well? Did you win?'

'Yes, yes, we won,' I reply.

Grandma's face lights up. 'Oh, Dr Krapotkin must be over the moon!' she says, clapping her paws.

168

'She is, but Grandma – there's something else. Something even more amazing happened. I met two other mice ... grown-up mice. A man one and a lady one. And they said to say "Hello" to you. And they also said not to tell anyone about them and I know it will sound strange but it felt ... well, it felt like they knew me.'

Grandma's face drops like I've just told her someone has stolen her tail. 'OK, you need to tell me EVERYTHING,' she says, recomposing herself, 'and then we will talk.'

So, I tell her all about V.E.R.M.I.N. and about getting ambushed by the

Mogg and about the return of Professor Armageddon and, then, how I ended up on the roof chasing him. Grandma listens intently, her eyes growing wider and wider as my story unfolds. 'And then,' I say, coming to the final, most important part, 'this mouse guy saved me from falling off the roof whilst this lady mouse knocked off all the cockroaches ... and when they left, the mouse guy said something strange about letting the power of the mouse guide me.'

Grandma takes a long, deep breath, like she's drawing all the air in the nest into her lungs. And then she says something so monumental that it literally takes all my breath away.

'Those mice,' she says, placing her paws on my shoulder, 'are your parents.'

My stomach turns a full somersault. My legs suddenly feel all wobbly, like they are made of water. 'They're ... they're **alive**?' I splutter. I have never once, in all my life, considered the possibility that they could still be living. 'I don't understand! You said they were dead.'

'I never said they were dead, I just said we couldn't talk about it,' she replies kindly, sitting down and patting the floor beside her. In a dizzy, confused heap I take my place next to her. 'I've never kept secrets from you, Stix,' she says, hugging me in close. 'I've just protected you from a truth that I didn't think you were ready to hear, or old enough to understand. But now you have seen what you've seen, it is time you knew.'

'They said they were from something called S.M.A.R.T.,' I add, suddenly remembering this important fact.

'Indeed, they are. Though they were once just young mice like you, until they were scouted. You see, S.M.A.R.T. is a top-secret organisation. It takes the very best, the most talented, most acrobatic mice, and it teaches them how to uphold our law.'

'S.M.A.R.T. came here, to the flat, and found Ma and Pa?'

'Well, we lived in Flat 2 at the time, but yes, yes, that's what happened. It is so rare to be chosen, especially two mice from the same family. But it's a call you can't refuse. The rule is you have to go, even if you have a new-born baby.' She looks at me, her eyes full of sorrow. 'It broke their hearts to leave you, but they did so in the knowledge that they would be making an invaluable contribution to our community and, of course, that I would take the very best care of you. Though I think them finding you on the roof, battling a mad cockroach, might have dented your mum's faith in me a little,' she chuckles.

'And will I see them again? Or is that it?' I ask, nervously.

'You will,' she replies, placing both paws on my shoulders. 'When a member of S.M.A.R.T. speaks their motto to you – and that is what your pa did when he whispered those special words in your ear – it is a sign that they deem you to have what it takes to join them. It is, in other words, an invitation.'

'They ... they want me to ... to be part of S.M.A.R.T.?' I stammer.

'Yes,' Grandma replies, a hint of sadness creeping into her voice. 'I suppose I've been hiding the truth from myself, pretending the day would never come. But it's always been clear to me that you inherited your parents' talents, and never more so than recently. Watching you doing all those daring things, I just knew ...' She lets out another one of her sighs and, suddenly, I understand.

She was not frustrated with me, just sad because she knew one day I would leave.

The thought of meeting my parents – of getting to spend time with them – fills me with unbelievable joy. But the idea of leaving home, of leaving my dear grandma, fills me with terror.

'Don't worry, you're young. It will be a while before you have to go. You're not escaping me and all my rules just yet.' She gives me a playful punch on the arm.

From the kitchen we hear the sound of Schnookums and Boo-Boo coming in for breakfast.

'Morning, Trevor,' Schnookums yawns loudly.

'My pho! My pho!' Boo Boo cries excitedly.

'Yeah, clever old Trevor found it the garden just now

when I took him out to do his business. Again!' replies MyLove.

'Sorry, Trevor had a bit of a blockage, but poo out now,' he woofs cheerily, though of course the mans don't understand a word he has said.

'Oh, well done! Good boy, Trevor, well done,' says Schnookums. 'Extra breakfast for you.'

'Yum!' woofs a very happy-sounding Trevor. 'Yum, yum, yummy, yum, yum.'

Grandma wraps her arms around me and gives me the biggest hug ever, and we fall asleep in each other's arms.

# THE NEW
# BEGINNING

When I wake everything feels normal and yet very
different. Something inside me feels complete, like I'm one
of Boo-Boo's jigsaw puzzles who has just found its missing
piece. Grandma seems changed too, like a weight has been
lifted from her. She even goes over and pats the sleeping
Trevor's bottom, thanking him for rescuing us from the bin
lorry.

On the fridge, I see Boo-Boo has drawn a picture of him
and surrounded it with heart shapes.

It's the weekend, which means no school and extra time

to play. As always, we have our supper and then Grandma heads back to the nest. Tonight, for the first time ever, she encourages me to practise my skills.

'Got to have you fighting fit,' she winks.

But I don't feel like doing anything. My head feels all kind of jumbly. It's full of thoughts about one day leaving the flat, of wondering how it will feel to say goodbye to Grandma, say goodbye to Batz, of how weird it will be to leave the world I know and enter a completely unknown one. But then I hear a soft thump and, moments later, a soot-covered Batz tumbles into the kitchen.

'Evening! Took the chimney,' she grins. 'I may be down, but I sure ain't out. What's on the menu for tonight, some Trevor-bottom jumping? Or maybe mix it up, do something else?'

Behind me I hear the
kitchen door creak open.
I spin around, ready to run
for cover.

'Er, hey.' Maximus waves
nervously, poking his head
into the room. 'Only me. Don't
worry, I've not come for the biscuits
this time.'

'I took pity on him ...' says Batz.
'Thought maybe we could show him
what having a good time looks like.
I mean, it's not exactly a barrel of
laughs down in the sewer.'

'What do you mean! It's lovely
down there,' snaps Plague One
defensively.

'Yeah, it's pitch black and it
stinks. What's not to love?' adds
Plague Two.

'Well, I'm just saying, he might

have more fun up here,' says Batz, 'but he's welcome to go back home if he wants.'

'Nah, I'll stay,' says Maximus. 'For a bit, you know, just to find out how lame your games really are.'

'Honestly?' I say, rolling my eyes. 'That's your only reason?'

'All right, maybe the sewer is a bit boring,' he says, grudgingly. 'And maybe I've decided you're not such a loser after all.'

'Well, isn't that just the sweetest thing anyone has ever told you,' Batz laughs, nudging me with her wing.

And, just like that, everything makes sense to me. One day I will leave Peewit Mansions and P.E.S.T.S. I will meet my parents and get to know them properly. But, for now, all that can wait. Because I've got important things I still need to do. Like having fun with my friends!

'OK then,' I say with a smile. 'Let's play hide and seek.'

# Join Stix and the other PESTS on more laugh-out-loud adventures!

Stix and Batz, I am not a clown!

Bestselling author **Emer Stamp** once had an overly long, pompous job title and worked in the Advertising industry. After carving out a successful career helping create, amongst other things, the famous John Lewis Christmas adverts — she decided, in 2015, to hang up her posh, pointy shoes and become a full-time author and illustrator. Since then, wearing only comfortable trainers, Emer has written and illustrated two series: **The Diaries of Pig** and **P.E.S.T.S.** Both have gone on to win awards and make her very proud. Her wish is to one day have a dedicated section in a book shop, but for now she's just very happy that you are holding one of her books in your hands.

If you'd like to see more of Stix and the PESTS gang, you can find them here ...

PESTS website: www.pestsbook.com

Emer's website: www.emerstamp.com

Emer's YouTube channel: The World of Emer Stamp

(Pssst ... Did you find the hidden message on the edge of the book? Check out the PESTS website for more secrets, games and all kinds of pesty fun. But remember, it's for **PESTS ONLY!**)